In the early '90s, a child was born. This child grew into a man-child and, like many his age, was surrounded with geek culture; fantasy, adventure, superheroes and legends.

Influenced and inspired, Luke MJ Powell hopes that he can become part of the culture that helped him become himself.

Dedication

To my mother,
For keeping me happy when skies were grey.

Luke MJ Powell

Vanicrast – Eclipse

AUSTIN MACAULEY PUBLISHERS™
LONDON • CAMBRIDGE • NEW YORK • SHARJAH

Copyright © Luke MJ Powell (2017)

The right of Luke MJ Powell to be identified as author of this work has been asserted by him in accordance with section 77 and 78 of the Copyright, Designs and Patents Act 1988.

All rights reserved. No part of this publication may be reproduced, stored in a retrieval system, or transmitted in any form or by any means, electronic, mechanical, photocopying, recording, or otherwise, without the prior permission of the publishers.

Any person who commits any unauthorised act in relation to this publication may be liable to criminal prosecution and civil claims for damages.

A CIP catalogue record for this title is available from the British Library.

ISBN 9781786933768 (Paperback)
ISBN 9781786933775 (E-Book)
www.austinmacauley.com

First Published (2017)
Austin Macauley Publishers Ltd.
25 Canada Square
Canary Wharf
London
E14 5LQ

Acknowledgements

To those who helped,
Thank You.

Chapter One
Game Announcement

The room outside the court was filled with disorder, camera pods floated in the air as reporters shouted over each other in an attempt to tell the latest news first; Kaio, the self-named 'God of Tournaments', had been captured that afternoon, and was already inside the court room facing judgement. Inside the court, order was being held by a thread. Kaio stood in the centre of the room, bound in chains that had been secured to the floor, every set of eyes firmly locked on him, analysing every move he made. The door at the back of the room opened, and Judge Franklin re-entered the court, Kaio smiled at the judge who refused to look at him. Once seated, Judge Franklin looked at the papers on his desk, and then addressed the room.

"Ladies and Gentlemen, we have now heard the events as told by those chosen to stand against Mr Kaio, and his games. We have heard how he kidnapped a total of one hundred and twenty-eight individuals and subjected them to mental and physical torture, which ended in over a hundred counts of assisted homicide. We have all witnessed the broadcasted footage, presented by Mr Kaio himself, of these games, without the ability to avoid viewership whilst in the presence of a television." The judge looked around the audience within the room, the families and friends of the victims, the police officers who had tracked down this individual, and the news reporters that had snuck in camera pods to film the trial, finally his gaze landed on Kaio. "So, Mr Kaio, what do you have to say for yourself?"

There was stillness at first. Anyone who had watched the judge speak now focused solely on Kaio. Kaio smiled. He slowly breathed in a large lungful of air, and then just as slowly, he breathed it out through his mouth. He stretched his mouth, rolled his tongue, and then proceeded to chew an invisible toffee.

"Mr Kaio, what do you have to say for yourself?" The judge repeated, becoming irritable at Kaio's obvious lack of respect. "Mr Kaio…" The judge was silenced by a loud clang, as all of the chains binding Kaio fell to the ground, passing through his body as if he wasn't there. Kaio rubbed his neck, rolled his shoulders and then spoke to the speechless audience.

"There are many who question how we came to be on this planet. Against what many elven supremacists believe, it has been discovered that humans were the first to walk upon the surface of Vanicrast." Kaio stepped forward, and flicked his wrist towards the ceiling; a ball of red light soared up from his fingers and expanded until it became a large screen, depicting images as he continued his speech, "Homo sapiens; young, naive, stupid, wandering around the surface and discovering many things that we now take for granted; order, fire, food… without humans, who knows what we would have become…" Kaio clapped his hands together and then threw his palms out across the floor, and as he did the bland tiles became a vibrant, holographic, sky view of ancient Vanicrast.

"Of course, scientific evolution isn't the only factor to our current variety of species. After the first fifty or so years of human development, Vanicrast was hit with shards of Estafer," The ceiling became the starry sky, with Vanicrast's moon sitting in the centre of the image, then just as suddenly as the picture had appeared, the large, crystallised dwarf-planet Estafer smashed into the moon. Estafer shattered into a million segments, and slowly began to fall towards the surface.

"These shards, or crystals as we've taken to calling them, burrowed themselves into Vanicrast, tainting the soil and water supply with mana."

"Mr Kaio, as astounding as this little show is, this has nothing to do with…" Judge Franklin began. Kaio calmly turned to look at him, the moment their eyes met, the sound was sucked out of the room, and the lights dimmed to near darkness. After a moment, Kaio broke eye contact, returning to his friendly charming appearance and breathing life back into the court, as the judge continued to stare blankly at the spot where Kaio had stood. Kaio continued,

"The surviving humans carried on, but soon those susceptible began to feel the effects of the crystals energy, and thus elves and warlocks were born. It's been a long time since then, and the crystals are still causing changes to the environment; once common house pets are transforming into beasts, whilst new species are still coming into existence as a cause of the perfect balance of science and magic in our atmosphere." The holographic world beneath Kaio's feet transformed as he talked, the plates shifting and changing until it was a reflection of the more recent version of Vanicrast.

"Yet, no matter how much we've changed, we still love one very human desire: the desire to destroy, and observe destruction. I mean look at Grothaig, one of the most beautiful, civilised countries turned into a graveyard filled with barbarians, purely because we didn't like the colour of our opposition's flags." The holographic Grothaig became alive with explosions, tree lines retreating and clearings blasting into existence in once complete areas of woodland. "We learnt from our mistakes though, since we unleashed the Hellfire." The moment the word left Kaio's lips, Grothaig burst into flames, the audience broke their silence for a moment, shocked by the sudden source of light, but the moment passed once they realised that there was no heat.

"A country burnt to ash, millions dead, a mistake that has knocked the world into a state of almost peace." The flames died, and the world continued to develop and change until it became a representation of the present Vanicrast.

"And yet, our desire is still very much alive, buried just beneath the surface, constantly being fed by our anger, envy, depression, jealousy, thirst for chaos, it grows daily with no sign of stopping until Grothaig happens again."

The floor set alight to the tune of Kaio's words, country after country, erupting into flame as Kaio foreshadowed a destructive future. Once the final inch of land was engulfed in fire, the hologram dissolved into nothingness, revealing the bland tiles beneath once again.

"That's why I hold my tournaments, not because I want to, not because I enjoy them, but because I need to, to save the planet I love." The audience began to nod in agreement, Kaio's words spinning around in their minds and helping them see from his point of view. Kaio lifted his fingers, and the camera pods the reporters had been attempting to hide whizzed towards him, halting once they captured him in a medium shot, the lighting changing to make for more dramatic footage.

"You have been watching my trial, and you have listened to my words. So, tune in on any television screen, plugged in or not, at 18.30 BCT, in two days, for the premier of the seventeenth season of *Eclipse*! I promise you will enjoy it!"

With a closing wink, the camera pods fell to the floor,
The lighting returned to normal,
The audience snapped out of their silent, dazed state,
And Kaio was gone.

Chapter Two
Thief for Hire

The short, balding human sat staring at the bottom of her boots; she often put her feet on the table like this, to remind her clients what she thought of them. The man sniffed, and wiped his cheek quickly with one hand as he held his tattered hat in the other, hoping to appeal to her sympathy, she smirked in response.

"I just," he stumbled, "thought that, if I got it, I'd be able to, to show my wife, I wasn't useless, you know?"

"No," she replied bluntly, lighting up a cigarette to give him another point of reference in the dark, basement office. "I've never had a wife, so I wouldn't know."

"No, of course, I didn't mean," he rushed, his foot in his mouth as he attempted to recover from his mistake, "I only meant... will you do it?" He swallowed, and she could hear him hold his breath as he waited for her answer. They always waited, they always prayed, her skill was legendary in the criminal world of Borantik, ever since she had stolen the central jewel from King Xavier's crown. She breathed in deeply, then blew out a ring of smoke at the shaking man, analysing his reaction, she could afford to be picky but he couldn't afford to lose her services.

"I want half," she stated, the smoke ring breaking when the bottom hit his throat. The man stared at her blankly for a moment, then slowly, her words sank in, his expression changed; resilient. He opened his mouth to argue, his brain caught his tongue, his brow softened, he tightened his lips, he swallowed, and then he nodded. She had won the argument without saying another word. "Come back tomorrow morning, six a.m., if you're late by more than five minutes, I keep it, understand? You will then cash it in, return and pay me my share. If you don't, I will take it all, understood?" The man nodded, and began the usual thank you song. She continued before she died from this boring ritual, "Get out."

She turned on the room's main light once the door had closed, she loved the showmanship of her profession; dark, mysterious to the outside world, a deadly balancing act inside. Reaching across the table, she opened the case-file once more; the golden war dagger of Higlo located in Higlo Inn, Elkanner. She had looked at the dagger multiple times in her travels and would often visited the inn for a pint after a mission in Elkanner, its location being close enough to the border to put her mind at ease if she got into any trouble. She took her feet off the table, and held her cigarette in between her thumb and forefinger, whilst she stared at the familiar schematics.

The inn had three obvious entrances: main door, back door and the door that led into the cellar. There were also, thirteen windows on the ground level; all unusable because of the inn's open floor plan, and twenty on the upper level; five in full view of the bar, five in full view of the lounge area, and the other ten leading into the ten rentable rooms; possibly occupied, with no way of knowing until she got someone to scope out the building. The dagger itself was located in the main lounge area, framed and hung on the wall opposite the bar, next to a framed letter from the Borantik armed forces explaining the daggers history.

She took a final drag before stubbing the cigarette out, and pondering her next step. Obviously, she would have to strike between the hours of one and two, when the sober were sleeping and the drunk were absent minded, meaning her only threat would be the innkeeper and her old friend, Hax Higlo. She clicked her neck, this mission was too personal, but the money was too good to refuse.

Slipping her arms into her jacket, she picked up her bag, a small black messenger bag filled with a maze of compartments by her own design. She rose to her feet, switching off the light, and then made for the door; it would take an hour to travel from Yanstag to Elkanner, giving her two hours to plan her strategy, assess the number of possible witnesses, and try not to get noticed by the police force that had plastered the main streets with wanted posters with her face and name on them.

***

Elkanner, Borantik's city of art, was surrounded by a river on both sides, which had kept it safe from previous assaults. She stood on the roof of Higlo Inn, the moon light betraying her near invisible presence. Below her slept three partners and six individuals, and below them roared a group of twelve drunken witnesses, celebrating a victory in a local Warrior Championship, Hax Higlo and a part-time staff member finishing their shift. She could feel the noise vibrate through the roof tiles and up her legs, making them a perfect cover for any noise she might make, but also making them the loudest bull horn if her actions were noticed.

She slithered her way to the edge of the rooftop, and sneaked a peek down at the main road: empty. Swallowing, she hung her legs over the edge and prayed that she'd calculated the momentum correctly, and that she had picked the correct window. Pausing only until she heard the loudest of cheers from the group below, she pushed herself off the edge, keeping her right hand clasped to roof so that she could turn her body, then in one clean motion, she kicked out her feet, released her grip and smashed through the window of the empty tenth room. She landed softly; the glass did not, rattling off of every surface that it had scattered on to.

There was silence downstairs; she held her breath, her ears darting to any sound in the building. Twelve dull thuds, followed by cheering, told her that they had quietened to partake in a drinking race, and were still focused purely on their own drunkenness. She breathed out a sigh of relief, and then advanced to the door, moving as quietly as her father's genes had blessed her with.

The inn hadn't changed since the last time she had been there, still dimly lit, with most of the profits going into Hax's other projects instead of back into the inn. Leaning over the banister, she counted her blessing as she realised that all twelve drinkers were stood at the bar, blocking Hax's view of the dagger, of course this also meant that if any of them looked, she would have no way of hiding herself whilst near the frame. However, she would cross that bridge if, or when, she had to.

Her eyes darted around the large room, before she put her hands on the banister and lifted her weight off the ground; the banister creaked a little in disagreement with the sudden pressure, but held her body mass willingly. After a comforting cheer from the crowd below, she slowly rose to her feet and edged her way around the banister, stopping just short of the bar's sidelines. Here she could either carry on round silently, then drop down in front of the frame, although this would put her at an elevated level, where the drunk's heads may not block her from Hax's busy eyes, or she could try something more risky. Rolling her shoulders, she knew that there was never really an option, and with one big push, she leapt from the banister; her mother would be proud.

She made contact with one of the tables, sending a pint glass flying, but the momentum forced her to continue her motion, hitting the ground and rolling forward, finishing behind a high backed armchair. Silence fell in the room. She heard one of the drunks question the noise. She heard Hax lift the barrier, intending to investigate. She heard him walk forward, his shadow looming over the armchairs shadow as he advanced. There was chuckling at the bar, Hax turned on his heels, then the drunks roared as one of their own was caught trying to pinch alcohol from behind the bar. Laughter, drinking, the air un-thickened as the room returned to its oblivious state.

Clinging to the floor, she weaved her way towards her target, darting from shadow to shadow, double checking the crowd behind her whenever she was in a concealed position. Her mind whirled with options if she was caught, but she quickly calmed these worries as she made her final advance to the frames.

Her eyes flicked over to the neighbouring framed letter:

Dear Mr H. Higlo,

It falls to me to inform you of the tragic loss; your brother, Commander Rinast Higlo, has fallen in battle. Commander Higlo lost his life whilst attempting to save the lives of innocent Grothaig civilians in a settlement near our main camp, who had not heard the Hellfire warning. Exact details are still under investigation, but his body was discovered two hours after the fires had died down. With how the bodies were found, it is currently believed that Commander Higlo had tried to shield a pair of children from the initial explosion. Due to this, and Commander Higlo's outstanding performance on and off the battlefield, please find enclosed Commander Higlo's golden war dagger. I hope you find some comfort from this. Your brother was a great man, and a brilliant soldier.

Kind Regards,
King Xavier

She had read the letter a few times before, but only now did she notice that the handwriting and the signature didn't match, it wasn't even the same ink. She shook her head, and turned toward the larger frame and its content.

It was a beautiful weapon, carefully crafted to show superiority, rather than to be used in the field of battle. She would have been surprised if a single drop of blood had christened the blade, or if the bull moulded pommel had hit anything other than Higlo's side. As her eyes glided over it, a small voice in the back of her mind questioned if half the profit was a worthy share. Blinking quickly, she placed her fingertips on the bottom corners of the frame and pushed up and out. She had practised for an hour on prototype frames, and discovered that this was the quickest and quietest way to get to the contents. A loud cheer behind her, caused her to apply more pressure, the bottom of the frame snapped, the dagger slipped out and penetrated the wooden floor audibly.

The room went silent; the group turned in unison and saw her, her back to them, wearing dark unisex clothing.

"Who the Zxaperia are…?" began the soberest of the crowd, but his question was cut short when she threw a needle into the air, smashing the closest light, plunging her side of the room into darkness.

The crowd rose to their feet. Hax ran around the bar, snatching up a crowbar en route. They all engulfed the room, searching every nook and cranny for the intruder. Hax yelled questions at the group about the thief, but they could only give vague details.

She stood for a moment in the doorway of Room Ten, the dagger securely inside the scabbard attached to her bag, as she watched their frantic, yet useless, search for the intruder. A look of smugness snuck onto her face as she closed the door, and leapt through the window into the cold night air.

***

She was sat behind her desk, smoking, when the short, balding human re-entered her office at six on the dot. The dagger was already on the table, waiting for its new owner. The man smiled at it before looking up at her. He reached inside his jacket pocket, and pulled out a police badge.

"Pandora Law, the sell-thief," the police officer began, "You are under arrest for property theft. You have the right to remain silent, anything you do say may be used against you in the court of law.

I've waited a long time to say those words."

Chapter Three
Let the Games Begin

A bright blue light exploded in the centre of the damaged throne room. Against the wall furthest from the door, a large blue crystal stood proudly, looming over the woman that had been teleported into the room. Pandora lay on her back, staring up at the blue sky through the gaps in the torn-up roof. She was no longer in the jail cell she had become familiar with over the last forty hours.

There was a crackling noise as some hidden machinery activated, then as she watched four images lit up parts of the remaining chunks of ceiling; a Sun, a Moon, and a zero underneath each symbol. Pandora tensed her abdominals, and pulled herself up into a sitting position, causing machinery to whir audibly as the next set of programmes was triggered by her movement. Pandora's eyes darted round the room; it was a disused throne room that seemed to have fallen to disrepair between age, and countless battles. Burnt banners littered the walls, covering holes and piles of rubble, each bearing the same Sun depicted on the ceiling.

A man flickered into existence by the door, unseen projectors struggling to keep up with his erratic movements. He was tall, wearing a black suit with red lapels, a black shirt and a thin red tie. His black hair, with blonde streaks, had been sloppily pushed back, showing his pointed ears and thin facial features: an elf. Yet, the skin around his fingertips and palms was stained black, an obvious trait associated with warlocks. Realising that the projection was rolling, the man stopped moving and focused forward.

"Warrior! Welcome, to Blue Crystal Island! I will be your host: Kaio, God of Tournaments, and you have been selected to play in this season's game of *Eclipse*!"

The man spoke happily, obviously struggling to contain his excitement. Pandora knew about *Eclipse*, and the gory ends many of its 'players' faced. Before she could voice her distaste of being kidnapped, and having her potential death broadcasted worldwide, Kaio continued, "Honoured, I'm sure. There are only two rules standing between you and your prizes. One, you and your team must take control of all nine landmarks on the island before facing me. In case you haven't noticed yet, I have attached a vanguard to your dominant arm, showing you a map of the island, where the capture points are, and the symbol of your team." Pandora looked at her forearm, noticing the thin, weightless, armoured material that had been secured to her right arm. Rotating her joints, she was surprised to note that this new addition didn't affect her movement, and instead bent and twisted with her skin, yet held fast when she attempted to remove it.

"The second rule, you may not leave the island whilst the game is in play; there's a two mile radius of safety, before penalties ensue. Other than that, feel free to do as you please, but make sure it's interesting, you're all on television. Good luck warriors, I'll be seeing some of you, very soon." The man vanished, while Pandora stared blankly at the wall behind him, processing the reality of her situation. She had been kidnapped, forced to take part in a murderous game of capture the flag, on a team of unknowns, for the entertainment of some warlock-elf hybrid, and the entire Vanicrast population.

"Wonderful," Pandora sighed, as she brought herself to her feet. When she extended to her full height, the machines whirred again, and Kaio reappeared, standing directly in front of her. "Holy…" Pandora began, jumping back. Kaio didn't react, but began his pre-recorded message.

"Welcome, to your new home Solar Team member, this is Sun Palace. This is your main base, and where you will respawn if you should be killed in the battlefield." Kaio stated, staring through Pandora, "The crystal currently contains five revives for your team, this means that each member of your team may die once without consequence. The flag for this location is located on the wall directly behind the respawn crystal. Good luck Team Solar, and be careful of the lava, I've cooled the heat it exerts, but it is very much real." With that closing bit of advice, Kaio disappeared again, and the machinery ran quietly, needing only to focus on the ceiling projections.

Pandora stared at the giant crystal that stood where the thrones would have been located. It was the largest shard of Estafer, she had ever seen, each face shimmering in the sun light, perfectly smoothed with strong edges skirting each of the imperfect sections. Pandora had doubted the stories of Estafer as a child, yet as she stared, she came to terms with the fact that this shard could not have been naturally formed on Vanicrast. Swallowing, she circled the crystal and discovered a plain white flag nailed to the wall. Cautiously, she reached out her hand, unsure of the consequences that this would have, and praying that this wouldn't be the first of many traps set up by Kaio. The moment her fingertips touched the material, the flag burst into a bright yellow with a crimson sun in the centre, matching the symbol on her vanguard. A trumpet blared out as the zero beneath the sun on the ceiling was replaced with a one.

Pandora smiled, her team was winning, for what it was worth. No sooner had the thought drifted through her head, the trumpet blared again, and the one changed to a two, whilst the zero under the moon turned into a three. Her smile evaporated, her victory short-lived, as the opposing team also realised that the flags weren't traps. Sighing, Pandora crossed the hall, and opened the doors.

It was the heat that hit Pandora first, and then the smoke, which wrapped its twirling fingers around her body, spiralling around her neck and pushing the clear air out of her windpipe as it travelled down into her lungs. Pandora retreated instantly, coughing violently as the smoke cleared. After a few moments, she looked at the open door, and watched the smoky steam creep up the opening, as if a sheet of glass was blocking its advances. Breathing slowly, ready for the sudden difference in atmosphere, Pandora stepped outside once more.

Directly outside the door was a thin stone bridge, with enough width for three people to stand shoulder to shoulder, with some difficulty as the bridge would concave and convex further down the long path. On either side of the bridge, bubbled Kaio's 'cooled' lava, happily rolling round the inside of the bowl beneath Sun Palace. It didn't take a genius for Pandora to realise that Kaio had thrown her into a decrepit building above a live volcano.

The possibility of becoming dazed from the smoke and falling to her fiery death was more than enough reason for Pandora to sprint the distance to solid land. Half way across, her left foot landed too close to the edge, loose stones gave out under her, her foot slipped down over the edge, her body followed. Pandora watched as her vision was suddenly dominated with the red, bubbling liquid, snatching at the air below her. As quickly as she had fallen into this situation; her right hand darted out, and Pandora's fingertips caught the uneven stone of the bridge edge. Her shoulder recoiled under the sudden pressure, but Pandora breathed easily, this hadn't been her first slip, nor would it be her last, if she could help it. Dragging herself back onto the bridge, Pandora continued at a more careful pace, keeping an eye out for loose stones and uneven levels, which desired to cause the trip that would end her life.

When she arrived at the end of the bridge, she fell to her knees for a moment; the physical turmoil and heat had taken its toll on her unexpectant body. As her lungs gasped greedily at the cool, smoke-free air around her, her eyes locked onto the horizon. A lone skyscraper stood over the tree tops, against a small mountain range background. As Pandora stared, something behind the mountain range launched skyward, rocketing up into the air, up through the clouds with no hint of slowing. Then as suddenly as it had appeared, the skyline burst into life in a shower of colour, as if a large firework had reached the peak of its journey and exploded.

Pandora pushed herself to her feet; to her right, another tower stood, yet as she watched, it seemed to shimmer and dance in the sunlight. Deciding on a direction, Pandora advanced toward the tower in front of her, favouring the more regular appearance on an island of madness.

It didn't take long for Pandora to stride into the small town between Sun Palace and the tower. The town looked as if it had been pulled out of an old Riodic history book; the dusty roads, the wooden buildings, the signs calling out to travellers about their content, and the horse posts with muddy drinking water. Pandora paused on the outskirts of the town, to read the sign above the entrance: Run-Down Town. A soft, cooling breeze pushed past her, and with it she heard a familiar mechanical sound before the holographic Kaio emerged beneath the sign, wearing a black cowboy hat.

"Yee-haw warrior, welcome to Run-Down Town. Funny story about this town; I purchased all the buildings and land, then transferred the entire town in from Riodic, doesn't get more authentic than that. The flag for this location is proudly flying in the centre of town, but is it your flag?" Kaio questioned with a cheeky smile before disappearing behind one of the entrance posts.

Pandora glanced at her vanguard, a Run-Down Town label had appeared under a red circle, similar to the one at Sun Palace. So, unless the vanguard was lying to her, one of her teammates had captured the town, and was possibly still within the town's perimeter.

Pandora stepped forward.

A patch of dirt exploded next to her foot.

The gun shot echoed.

A figure whistled from a nearby balcony, a rifle trained on Pandora.

"The next shot won't miss," the figure called. "Who are you? And what is this place?"

Chapter Four
Nightfall

"Good luck warriors, I'll be seeing some of you, very soon." Kaio finished before crackling out of existence, revealing the scorch mark on the wall from the fire blast Gronix had instinctively thrown. He was sat on a round table in the centre of the courtyard, surrounded by tall, black stone walls, with complimentary towers in each corner. Gronix turned his head to examine this unfamiliar location; a large wooden drawbridge stood in front of him, with four images on either side of the entrance, a sun and a zero on one side and a moon and zero on the other. Behind him proudly stood a miniature castle, holding a large, blue crystal that the castle had been built around, and a regular sized flag of surrender waving above it.

Gronix immediately recognised the crystal as an Estafer revival shard, similar to the ones found in the Yanstag's Mana Academy. Gronix wiped his eyelids with blackened fingertips, and muttered a spell that he had read but never used. Removing his hand from his face, he stared out with peacock blue eyes, and surveyed the area once more. He made out the outline of several small machines hidden in the walls; he was able to distinguish the invisible markings on the floor for where Kaio's holograms were set, and the large, white circle from where the crystal had spawned the deceased players of games past. Looking down below his feet, he noticed a thin, invisible mist covering the ground, attached to another machine, ready to activate the next hologram. Gronix sighed, blinking viciously until his eyes returned to their natural colour, and then slipped off the edge of the table. Sure enough, he heard one of the machines boot up, and Kaio appeared a few inches away from Gronix.

"Welcome, to your new home Nocturnal Team member, this is Nocturnal Castle. This is your main base, and where you will respawn if you should be killed on the battlefield." Kaio stated, staring through Gronix. "The crystal currently contains five revives for your team, this means that each member of your team may die once without consequence. The flag for this location is located on top of the castle. Good luck Team Nocturnal, and be careful of the river, it's connected to the outside water supply, and filled with the beasts that roam the waters in this area." With that closing bit of advice, Kaio disappeared again, and the machinery ran quietly, needing only to focus on the wall projections.

Gronix rubbed his hands together, and assessed his situation silently; a homicidal game to capture territory. Gronix smiled, this kidnapping may be a blessing in disguise; a place where he could practise all of the new spells he'd gathered in his travels without prejudice, as he would only be trying to survive what many would perceive as a nightmarish situation. Turning he stared at the white flag, blowing unnaturally in the still air, he circled the castle slowly watching its movements. It was obvious that a minor spell had been cast on the flag to keep it moving, but he couldn't remember a spell that would help him identify if any traps had been cast on the material. When he reached the back of the castle, there was a soft clicking sound as the zero under the sun changed into a number one; he was on the losing team.

Gronix despised the idea of losing, snapping his hand shut, he caught the flag between his fingertips. One of the machines blurted out a heartfelt trumpet, as the white material transformed into a dark blue, with a cream moon symbol in the centre, replicating the one on the wall, and on his unwanted vanguard. The zero quickly turned into a one, and then a three as the trumpet tooted twice more, whilst the Solar's score clicked into a two. Gronix would win this game, or die trying.

***

Gronix hadn't thought about Kaio's closing statement until he was stood in the centre of the wooden drawbridge between the castle and the meadow on the opposite bank. The moment the drawbridge had landed, Gronix had heard a new noise mixed with the quiet breeze that had rolled in, a soft running water sound that alone was deceptively calming but was accompanied by the distinctive dual fins of Rip Jaws breaking the surface of the murky water inside the moat.

Gronix had read stories of Rip Jaws, how they could sense movement from ten miles away, and how they'd been known to tear trucks apart because they didn't recognise the truck's motions. He crouched, hypnotised by the circling, how the fins danced through the surface of the water. The only things between him and certain death were approximately 2 feet of wood and 6 inches of air, Gronix swallowed, unable to tell if this experience was exciting or unnerving.

He watched as a pair of fins advanced then submerged, naturally Gronix turned to watch the fins resurface, but they never did, turning back, Gronix had to catch his heart in his throat as the Rip Jaw stared blindly at the warlock. Gronix felt his blood freeze in his veins as he stayed motionless. There were few things in Vanicrast that could cause such a reaction, but Gronix was yet to witness anything that deterred from the stories he had read about these powerful, cold-blooded water demons. Gronix stared into the creature's eyeless sockets, attempting to read its face for any hint at an appropriate reaction, unable to assess how much of a threat it really was.

After a few minutes, the Rip Jaw re-submerged; Gronix breathed a sigh of relief and hastened off of the bridge, suddenly feeling vulnerable. He had always hated water, its reflective properties being a nightmare when casting spells. When he reached the bank, Gronix assessed the three dirt paths before him; to the north was a forest, whilst the east path led towards short mountains and a large thin tower, and the south led between the mountains towards a small building, with a partially domed roof, on the other side of the valley. As he weighed up his options he noticed a small winged figure hurtle up through the air, hitting the clouds at a break-neck speed, followed by a massive explosion.

His ears rang out as he watched body parts and feathers float down. It was plenty enough reason for Gronix, so he made a ninety degree turn and began his journey towards the woods. Glancing at his vanguard, he noticed that the north and south locations had been captured by his team; the south location was named Dreamers Observatory, whilst Gronix was heading towards War Forest.

The forest looked like it had come out of Grothaig prior the war; tall, beautiful trees, thick bushes and wildlife audibly roamed throughout the woodland. When Gronix past the first five or so trees, the familiar machine noise came to life and Kaio stood before him, wearing a skirt made of leaves over his suit.

"Welcome warrior, to War Forest. The flag for this location is within the most northern area of the forest, attached to one of the oldest and tallest trees in Vanicrast, and a little advice warrior; be careful where you step, some of the wildlife can really stop you in your tracks." Kaio smiled, then grabbed a holographic vine and swung behind a tree. Gronix immediately got the feeling that these pre-recorded messages would be located at each of the capture points, making them simultaneously a courtesy and an annoyance.

Gronix began travelling north and soon felt multiple eyes watching him. Rubbing his hands together, he lit them on fire, warding off any would-be attackers, but he could not shake the feeling. Burning through a tangle of vines, Gronix found himself in a small clearing, and faced against three fully grown Murder Pups, woken by the unusual crackling sound made by the heated greenery. The beasts rose to their full height, growling loudly whilst baring their double rows of pointed teeth, attempting to put the fear of god into him.

Gronix swallowed, this would be the first time to practise, yet his mind was blank, and he could only think of the first dark spell he'd learnt. How powerful it had made him feel, and how long it had taken his victim to bleed out before death finally took hold. He raised his left hand and the dogs' growls were silenced, fear made the air thick around them. He opened his right hand slowly; the dogs obediently opened their mouths, their eyes widened as they felt the control of their own bodies slip away from them. Then, in one slow motion, Gronix turned his right palm to the sky and brought the tips of his fingers together. Synchronised with Gronix's action, the dogs' mouths spewed out their organs, until their insides were outside of their bodies. Gronix stared at the feral beasts as he returned bodily control to them, and they could only whimper as they stared at the intruder who had dispatched them so easily. After an age, the blood loss sank in, and one by one, the Murder Pups shut their eyes and accepted the welcoming embrace of nothingness. Gronix passed the corpses, the encounter had been inconvenient, but it was always good to put his learning to practice.

Stepping forwards back into the woodland, Gronix felt something graze his leg, the wispy sensation of a spider's web breaking as it made contact with his shin. When his foot hit the ground, it gave out beneath him; suddenly Gronix was on the ground staring up at the patches of sky behind the treetops.

He had fallen victim to another creature he had only experienced in stories.

Descending towards him was a red arachnid, specifically an Orákon:

The paralysis spider.

Chapter Five
A Quick Bit of History

Kaio rubbed his palm with his thumb, tracing the pale scar from his time in Grothaig. He was sat in his office in Kaio Mansion, on a small offshore island to the northeast of Blue Crystal Island. In front of him were eight television screens, each linked to invisible camera pods perfectly trained on the six remaining players of the game, and in the centre was a large analogue clock, partially painted red to help Kaio remember the broadcasting time. Licking his lips, Kaio stood and made his way to his green room. As he walked he looked out of the window at Blue Crystal Island, his creation, and pondered how much he was really helping.

Since he began the games, worldwide crime and death rates had halved, nobody wanted to make their presence too well known, for the wrong reasons, in fear of being chosen to play, unknowing that it made no difference. Kaio didn't spend time selecting his players; he didn't have a complex system where he would choose one person from each area of Vanicrast. All he did was blindly throw darts at a tumbling globe, and whoever was there in the real world was teleported into the game; pure random selection.

As he entered the green room, the timer began to count down to broadcast time. The camera pod was already staring at him as he closed the green door. The creatively named green room, held no furniture, and all of the walls were covered in a thick, even green paint, making it easy for Kaio to change the environment at his leisure; film makers had learnt how to do it digitally, Kaio had taken it a step further. As he waved his hand to the floor, a replica of his throne from the office materialised, changing into the rich red and golden colour similar to his original. The timer began to chime as Kaio sat down, the background transforming into an overlook of Blue Crystal Island, it would have been less effort to film on the roof, but here Kaio had complete control over the lighting, the weather, the colours, everything that the audience could witness, was first filtered through Kaio. The timer stopped, and the camera began to broadcast.

"Ladies and Gentlemen, welcome to the seventeenth season of *Eclipse*. As always, I am your host, Kaio, God of Tournaments." Kaio smiled, and the fake audience cheering track activated, he let it play for a few moments, creating a few camera flashes to help with the illusion, before continuing, "Now, as always, I have gotten eight random individuals from the outside world and brought them into the newly redesigned Blue Crystal Island, and put them in the two teams: Team Solar and Team Nocturnal." Raising both of his hands palms up, the symbols of each team appeared to hover above them.

"Now, the players have only been in the game for two hours, and already we have some amazing highlights for you, but before we get to that, I have a question for you all. What shall I name this creature?" As Kaio asked, he put his hands together and the two symbols merged to create a small octopus-humanoid creature, with red markings on its face and upper body. "I discovered it whilst terraforming the island, the effects of the crystals creating yet another species for our world. So, any suggestions?" Kaio paused, listening to the entire population as they screamed at their televisions.

"We have a winner: Effaid Traol! You will find a Kaio coin under your pillow in the morning; try not to spend it all at once. From now on, these little water demons will be recorded as Kylocks. A fitting name, I do believe." Clapping his hands together, Kaio stood up with a smile, as the throne melted behind him.

"Now, before today's highlights, I feel that we should look back on how far we've all come, a quick history lesson, if you would. Today, we are celebrating the fifth year of *Eclipse*, and the tenth anniversary of the Grothaig Hellfire conclusion. I hope you're as proud as I am; ten years without even the hint of war in the air, and all of our nasty desires for destruction settled through media outlets. I want to remind you of our first season of *Eclipse*, five years ago," The island behind Kaio shrank and transformed into a circular land with trees in the middle, the tower still in the centre, and sand along the shorelines, "I was rocking a Mohawk and shoulder pads, and you guys didn't even know my name, but in that first game I brought players from all backgrounds, I brought in a king, a war chief, two assassins, a murderer, and a litter of less interesting characters, and you all watched. Sure, I didn't give you much choice, but you still watched, with many of you travelling miles to get to a television to view recordings of this original spectacle." Kaio's eyes glazed momentarily, nostalgic of how far he'd come in such a short period of time.

"Of course, the editing and camera work was sloppy; the island was uninhabited and far too small, and the game didn't even last a single night. Learning curves, am I right?" The island behind him snapped back to the present incarnation, "Five years later, I'm still getting a mismatch of players, and you lot are still watching with open eyes.

"Now, this is the first season of this year, and as always, you decide how many seasons there will be, and not by shouting at your TV, Effaid Traol. If you want more seasons, you just have to show your violent streaks, and if you want to watch less people die on your television screens, then continue being the peaceful populations, I know you can be.

"You may now be curious why I'm still talking, what this has to do with history, and why this season has started if you were being peaceful, and the truth is, some of you aren't being peaceful. I don't select the players, but I know the culprits; the ones who are planning to rid Vanicrast of its world leaders by violent means, killing many innocent civilians in the process. So, I'll now remind you all of our third year of *Eclipse*, when I held seven seasons to satisfy the thirst of a certain war-chief before he executed a plan to destroy a capital city. I didn't want to hold that many seasons, I don't want to hold that many seasons again, but I will repeat my actions if I must. Don't make history repeat itself," Kaio stared sternly into the camera lens, "This is your final warning."

Kaio held the silence for a beat longer than was comfortable, and then broke his lips into a smile.

"With all that sorted, shall we talk about the games?"

The fake audience cheered, "So, this time round, I've separated the teams and put one player near the flag that they'd be able to capture the easiest. This is as an act of generosity, and to speed up the beginning of the game, which would always drag when they spent hours on end travelling from one flag to the next. Now, so far Team Nocturnal is in the lead with three flags, but Team Solar is right on their heels with two. However, the really interesting bit is that two of our competitors have already been pulled out of the competition! I know! You want to watch? Well, don't worry; coming up next is the highlights of each player, and the deaths of two of our late competitors. Enjoy!"

Kaio turned invisible, and the background zoomed around the island.

A forest covered in blood.

A maze full of fog.

A winged figure stood in front of a mountain of rocks.

Kaio left the room silently, pondering, *how much help was he really doing?*

Chapter Six
Rule Breakers

Almar stood below a tall rock formation inside a deep canyon, a white flag waved proudly at the top of the stone tower. The holographic man had informed her of the situation, and she had tried to tear his head off, becoming enraged when her sharp nails had passed through his electronic presence. Almar looked at the barren surroundings, this canyon was unnaturally made, and it did not sit well with her. Stretching her wings, Almar screeched up to the sky, investigating if any more of her kind were in the area. She waited, her wings twitched and warmed, but no answer came.

Almar stepped forward. She did not enjoy the sensation of hot rock under her bare feet. As her foot hit the ground, the holographic man returned, mockingly sporting a small pair of angel wings similar to what a human would wear to a fancy dress party. Almar immediately leapt at him, extending her fingers to drive her talons into his throat, but again, she passed through him harmlessly.

"Welcome Warrior, to Famine Valley," the holographic man said, staring at where Almar had stood. "The flag for this location is on top of the formation behind me, the highest point inside the valley, but don't go too high, don't forget the rules." Finishing, the man looked up then sank into the ground, Almar spat on the patch of soil where he'd disappeared. She had not become a Queen to be kidnapped and ordered around like a hatchling.

Extending her wings, Almar crouched down then launched herself into the air. The roar of the wind was welcoming to her stressed mind, as she rocketed past the flag and continued upwards. She would not partake in this game, or its rules; she had a city to lead.

The holographic man reappeared when she broke through some clouds, but in physical form. He raised one hand, and Almar stopped in the air.

"Queen Almar of Harkall, if you continue, you will be breaking the rules." He spoke coldly, with an edge of encouragement. "There will be consequences for these actions if you do not descend and participate in the tournament." Almar screeched at the man, desiring to strike out at him but unable to move her suspended body. The man sighed, lowering his hand before he dissolved into the clouds, as he did; Almar was returned control of her levitating body, which dipped momentarily as her wings sluggishly awoke and kept her from falling to her demise.

'Consequences' rattled round Almar's head, there would be 'consequences' if she didn't play, but there would be 'consequences' if she did; her people had never been without a leader, and she had not done the things she'd done to gain her power, only to give up her position to play some minor game of murder.

Almar continued on her upward path, and then the consequences began. It was a minor sensation at first, a small amount of heat inside her stomach, which burned quickly until Almar screeched in pain, and then the feeling stopped.

Almar's eyes glazed, her mind fizzled out, then she exploded.

Nothing was revived,
The blue crystal hummed quietly.
She had faced the consequences of her actions,
Queen Almar was dead.

***

Kors lay under the surface of the rippling water, on a shallow bank, a few feet away from the waterfall that ran from the sky, and looked like an infinitely tall tower of water. The properties in the pool were not the same as those in Ingswa; his scaled flesh had lightened to the warmer water. Kors rolled his wrists and his ankles, feeling the water swirl around his webbed fingers and toes. Kicking out, he darted into the centre of the pool with ease, and examined his new submerged surroundings beneath the pool's tiny island. The moment he reached his destination, something reached him.

Small tentacles latched onto his leg, its strange octopus-humanoid head staring up at him, smiling widely with a strangely menacing toothless grin. As Kors watched, the small creature raised its two sharp hind-tentacles, and positioned them to strike his stomach. Moving quickly, Kors punched the creature in the face, as his other hand snatched a Rip Jaw tooth he had hidden between his lower back scales. The creature repelled, growling as it tightened its grip on his leg, before Kors brought the tooth down into the little monster's skull. It froze immediately, its eyes clouding red as blood gushed out of its brain, leaked into its skull. Kors pried the beast off, as his eyes spotted more of its kind swimming towards him. Once he was free, Kors torpedoed towards the surface, breaking through with enough force to leap to the grassy bank effortlessly.

When his feet hit the grass, a machine clicked on and a suited man appeared, explaining that his name was Kaio, he was a 'God', and that Kors had been selected to play in a televised game called '*Eclipse*'. Once the man had finished, Kors looked back at the pool. The water seemed deceivingly clear, yet Kors now knew what dwelled below the surface. In the centre of the pool was a tiny, sandy landmass, with just enough space for a coconut tree and plain flag. Moving round slightly, Kors noticed that the pool had created a small river that headed towards a giant tower, south-west of his location. Kors turned to look offshore, and saw another small island, this one housing a grand mansion, a massive satellite dish and a runway with a selection of light aircraft.

Stepping towards it, Kaio reappeared wearing a pair of swimming goggles and flippers, clashing greatly with his suit.

"Welcome warrior, to Endless Falls," Kaio smiled, "Interesting fact, the name is literal, as the waterfall is formed by water particles in the air, once they touch the net of magical energy I've created, the particles multiply and become water, making it fall constantly. The flag for this location is in the centre of the pool, but watch out for the Kylocks inside the water; they've only just been discovered." With that Kaio jumped into the pool, creating a holographic splash.

Kors looked from the mansion to the flag, and then dived into the water.

***

The tiled floor was slippery beneath Kors's feet, but he knew how to end this game quickly. He could hear Kaio rehearsing his words for the first live broadcast, some drivel about how peaceful Vanicrast is. Another powerful person ignoring the attacks Ingswa was subjected to daily by the barbaric forces of Grothaig.

He crawled up the stairs, his scales darkening as they dried, limiting his athletic movement as they hardened into light armour. Kors drew another Rip Jaw tooth from the other side of his lower back as he rounded the corner to a long hallway with windows along the entirety of one side. Kors heard a flush before Kaio emerged from a door two-thirds of the way up the hall. He had his back to Kors, as he unknowingly returned to his office, leaving the door open. Kors moved silently, reaching the door before Kaio was comfortable in his office throne. Kors readied himself for his attack, rolling the tooth between his fingers.

"Are you going to stand out there all day, Kors?" Kaio called, "You realise I have to start broadcasting in… an hour." Kors's blood froze, how did Kaio know? He was able to sneak up on a Rip Jaw, and remove their teeth, without them ever knowing he was there.

"Need a little encouragement?" Kaio asked, "Fine, let me help." Kors feet were lifted off the ground, and he was brought into the office.

On the wall were eight screens around a large clock, each screen following the eight players of Kaio's game.

On one of the screens was Kors; hovering helplessly in front of his kidnapper. Kors turned his head and stared Kaio in the eyes, unafraid.

"You broke the rules, Kors Edria, soldier of Ingswa. And rules can be seen as orders." Kaio stared back, acknowledging Kors' fearlessness. "And breaking Ingswa orders is punishable by death."

"Then do it," Kors roared, he refused to have this honourless death prolonged.

"Fine," Kaio replied, clicking his fingers.

Kors vanished with a deafening crunch.

Kaio looked at one of the screens, sighed then vanished too.

The room was silent.

Many of the screens lit up, as if a firework had been caught on several camera pods.

Kaio reappeared in his seat.

"This will be a very interesting season."

Chapter Seven
War Forest

Murados lay in a bed of dried leaves with her eyes shut, as she felt a bug crawling across her bare neck. As the pest paused on her throat, she slapped her hand to her neck and peeled the little insect corpse from her flesh, her eyes snapping open as her skin began to burn. Dangling from her fingertips was a Blue Preacher, its corrosive blue blood dripping onto her burning neck. In one fluid motion, Murados screamed in pain and dropped the large spider into her mouth, swallowing it quickly. The effects occurred instantaneously, her neck healed, her veins became more prominent and her spine snapped and grew as her legs multiplied. Spinning her lower appendages and using the momentum, Murados leapt to her feet.

"Warrior!" A voice began, Murados reacted instinctively biting into her wrist and spraying her blood towards the voice. The hologram continued, "Welcome, to Blue Crystal Island! I will be your host; Kaio, God of Tournaments, and you have been selected to play in this season's game of *Eclipse*!" Before Kaio could continue to an audience, Murados's instincts had reacted again, her legs speeding towards the nearest tree. Reaching the treetop, she could still hear the holographic Kaio rambling on below her. Murados knew of '*Eclipse*', the games and reactions had been plastered on every television she'd ever encountered, for as long as she could remember.

As she surveyed her new surroundings from her elevated level, she spotted a white speck flicking in her peripheral vision. Turning, Murados's eyes latched onto a white flag swaying in the breeze at the peak of a gigantic tree, its thick trunk overlooking the entire woodland area. Her body moved before her brain could react, the Blue Preacher genes screaming at her to get to higher ground whilst she still felt vulnerable. Her legs moved gracefully, bounding from branch to branch like it was a dance, two of her 'feet' supporting her weight as another two stretched for the next twig.

She reached the flag in mere minutes, the reflective surface mesmerising her as it waved in the wind. She licked her lips as she extended her fingers to touch the material, ready to strike if that was what was needed. As she did, another object attracted her attention, something attached to her forearm; it was brown and stretched over her recently transformed appendage, with a strange moon branded close to her wrist and a map covering the top of her forearm. Murados stared at it intensely, examining this strange addition to her person, then one of the white markings turned red, and something triggered inside of her. In one smooth motion, Murados opened her mouth as wide as she could, and then she buried her face into her bicep, her fangs hacking through skin, muscle tissue and bone.

The severed limb hit the solid earth with a thud, having bounced off of every branch on the way down, the blood burnt its way through the living wood as it attempted to follow the appendage to the ground. Murados watched as the bone re-grew, the blue veins wrapping around the bone, altering their state to become muscles, skin tissue, and soon her arm had fully grown back, but between blinks, the vanguard reappeared too. Murados lashed out in her frustration, her fingers splitting open on the rough bark, and corroding the wood beneath. Reaching upwards, Murados stretched out her fingers toward the disgustingly, blinding white flag, intending to melt it, but as her fingers touched the material, the flag was set alight with colour; starting from where her fingers had met the material, the white burned away and was replaced with a deep calming blue, until it reached the centre and the blue wrapped around a pale moon symbol like the one on her unwanted vanguard.

Murados's eyes were fixated on this strange flag, its reactive properties mimicking her own abilities on a minor scale. She could feel something from her past trying desperately to bubble to the surface, something from before the operation, something before her death...

An explosion behind her snapped her out of her trance, a tear rolled down her cheek as the incomplete memory dissolved back into nothingness, and she was left with nothing but the emptiness she knew too well. She turned, and watched blood and feathers fall from the clouds like confetti, between small, distant mountain peaks. Behind the valley was a tower that stood like a powerful sceptre and, Murados imagined, could be seen from anywhere on the island.

As her eyes wandered across the horizon, she spotted a man walking towards the forest, his black hair moving with each stride. Murados licked her lips as her mouth salivated; a delicious meal was walking towards her. She leapt from her branch, and fell towards the ground, her legs stretched out to catch a branch before she collided with the earth, but as she fell, her hands wrapped around a much tastier alternative for her journey.

***

Murados watched the man with unblinking eyes; he wore a large, thin cloak, that hid his torso from her, and black suit trousers that gave her no hint of who this person was. His hair had been pushed out of his face, but it fell around the sides mocking his attempt to keep it out of his eyes on a long-term basis. Murados had tasted his kind before; the black hair and blackened palms screaming volumes to her stomach; warlock.

As if he heard her thoughts, the warlock rubbed his hands together and they set ablaze, the flames crackled in her eyes as she watched him enter a Murder Pups sleeping pit. Before she could let out a sigh of regret at the prospect of losing a meal, the warlock pulled the Pups organs out through their mouths. The act of gory violence brought a smile to Murados's lips, it was beautiful. The warlock continued north, and then collapsed, caught in a trap by an Orákon. She watched as it began to descend on its prey and considered her options, the Wobok meat finally settling in her stomach.

In one speedy swoop, Murados soared between the trees and snatched the little spider out of the air, crushing it in her talons as she landed a few feet from the paralysed victim. She patted herself on the back as she advanced; she had never been very graceful with her landings, never having wings long enough to overcome the learning difficulties. Murados was soon standing over the man, her wings tucked behind her neatly, the inside of her mouth flooding as she observed the food she had been served. Her eyes locked on to the accessory attached to his wrist, and then with a scowl, she spat at the man.

"What the Zxaperia?" the man shouted, leaping to his feet as he wiped his face of saliva.

"Would you have preferred to stay on the ground?" Murados replied coldly, the man fell silent as he realised what had happened.

"What are you?" he asked, examining her, "You don't look like any breed of Harkall I've ever seen."

"And no warlock I've ever seen would have been caught by an Orákon," She was beginning to regret her decision, "But as luck may have it, Woboks can cure most poisons, meaning you aren't being slowly devoured. You're welcome."

"I never asked for your help," venom dripped from his words.

"And I never asked to save you from an incy wincy spider," Murados replied mockingly, "But you and I seem to have a similarity that I don't understand." She raised her vanguard, holding it still so that the warlock's eyes could focus on the same moon that was on his vanguard.

"So, you're a player too, huh?" he asked rhetorically, before nodding, "Good, you seem useful." He extended his hand, "Gronix, let's see if we can't win this little game, shall we?"

Murados stared at his hand, then smiled, "Murados, and I think that I shall." With that she brought her talon fingers to her lips, slipped the Orákon into her mouth, and then took Gronix's hand as she swallowed.

Gronix's eyes widened as Murados transformed in front of him, her wings detaching and falling to the ground, her talons retreating into her fingers that kept a tight grip on his hand, and then her legs split into three pairs, as her joints developed a deep, blood red complexion. When her mutation had completed, she stared into Gronix's eyes and opened her mouth. He knew the look well and reacted quickly, twisting his body and smashing his free hand into her wrist, snapping it on impact.

Murados screamed in pain, which quickly changed to anger, as Gronix retreated from his attacker. Gronix had read many volumes, containing stories of shape-shifters who were able to take the form of an animal under the right conditions, but they had always been strictly held between two forms; humanoid and animalistic. Gronix had never even heard a fictitious tale that included anything like Murados had just demonstrated. As he fled, he could hear her trample the undergrowth as she chased him. Clapping his hands together, his body split into three copies, each never breaking stride.

Murados screamed as the trio parted, each sprinting down different pathways. Picking the closest path, she gave chase, weaving between trees elegantly before Gronix tripped on a tree root, and Murados' leg pierced through his chest. Murados chuckled as she brought her meal up to her drooling lips, but before her teeth could sink into her prize, Gronix began to dissolve into the air he was created from.

The true Gronix sat in a purple hexagon, and chanted quickly, hearing Murados yell in anger as she realised his deceit. Grabbing the rim of his sleeve, Gronix unthreaded some stitching and put it in his mouth, letting it soak in his saliva, as he continued the chant. Murados's figure whizzed past the bush in front of him, chasing after the second copy; he was running out of time. Baring his teeth, the chant grew louder and faster, but Murados's figure slowly returned. Gronix stared at the figure as it pushed its way through the shrubbery, and soon their eyes were locked onto each other. Murados rose up one of her legs, readying herself for the kill that she desired. As the sharp 'foot' fell, Gronix opened his mouth; the chant finished.

A black hand burst from Gronix's mouth, catching Murados's attacking limb, then it twisted, ripping the leg from Murados's body. Screaming, she retreated, staring horrified at the arm as it dug her leg into the ground and used it to pull its way out of Gronix. A second hand emerged, stretching Gronix's mouth, as it dragged itself out, soon there was a head and staring red eyes glaring back at Murados, and then a torso, and then… nothing. The demon hovered above the ground, its body stopping after its abdominal muscles. Its skin was burnt black like the warlock's palms, but with red lines covering its body, outlining its muscle structure to make it look as powerful as it seemed, whilst a detached red rings pattern wrapped around his wrists like cuffs.

Murados snarled at the demon, who stared at her.

"Omiss," Gronix said, wiping blood from his mouth, "Kill her."

Omiss looked at Murados blankly, and then, the tips of his lips twitched and soon he was smiling with his sharpened teeth on display. Murados held her ground, ready for an attack.

"Wait!" shouted an unseen, feminine voice from above the trio. A robotic figure stood on a tall branch looking down on them; its unmoving mouth contained the speaker the voice was coming from. "Instead of killing each other, let us join forces and claim victory. You are both very powerful beings, as we've witnessed, and there is little point in proving it here. Come to Dreamer's Observatory, and I can show you what I've learnt, and the people we have been opposed with."

Omiss looked at Gronix, who held out a hand to pause his murderous advance.

Murados's eyes darted between the three figures, unwelcoming of the ideas of death or alliance.

The robot stared down on them, expressionlessly.

"Follow the robot!" The speaker shouted, as the robot fell to the ground and turned south. "I will be waiting to meet you." As the robot turned, the trio spotted a 'R2' branded its body.

Gronix stared at the robot as it walked, then at Murados, who shared his curious yet vicious expression. Swallowing, he made the first move, walking past Omiss towards the robotic figure.

Omiss followed his summoner's lead.

Murados stared at the trio then followed, her belly grumbling.

Chapter Eight
Blood Stone Maze

Trigger woke in a small town, which reminded nem of nir home town in Riodic. Something screamed more than nostalgia though, the way the jail house walls concaved, the way that most of the horse posts hung too low to securely tie off a horse, and how the thick layer of red paint covered the house in front of nem, screamed volumes. Stepping into the wooden structure, ne advanced quickly to the main bedroom, and there ne discovered it; a small red hand print with nir name scrawled next to it. This did not just remind nem of nir home, it was nir home.

Trigger stumbled out of nir house; falling off the porch that ne had helped paint in nir youth. Ne remembered the way the paint had stuck to nir hands for days, how the smell had clung to nir skin for weeks. Nir head span as ne looked for any signs of life, but it was evident that nothing had touched these dusty tracks in years. Ne couldn't begin to guess the time lapse between when ne left and the time ne was in now – fifty years? A hundred? A thousand lifetimes? Tears threatened to escape nir eyes as nir mind drifted between the faces ne'd left behind when ne had trapped nemself in

Vilderton.

As ne rose to nir feet, a piece of modern technology clicked on, and a holographic man appeared out of thin air. Trigger went for nir empty holsters, but settled quickly, this wasn't nir first meeting with electronic men. The man introduced himself to Trigger, as Kaio, and then proceeded to tell nem the situation: Blue Crystal Island, *Eclipse*, capture the flags. It was a simple yet deadly premise that ne did not want to be part of. As suddenly as the man appeared, Kaio disappeared, and Trigger ran towards the mayor's office in the centre of town. Everything looked the same to nem; the creaking raised panel doors to the saloon, the whistling as the winds blew through the barbers, the echoing of the flag strings bouncing off of the town flagpole. Nir eyes drifted up to the flag, expecting to see the nostalgic Venom Dust Biter insignia on a red and black background, but instead ne discovered a white banner flourishing in the air.

Ne scowled at the flag of surrender that hung over the town. Without thinking, ne strolled to the flagpole and untied it, pulling down the shameful sight that mocked nir memory. As ne pulled the material away from the pole, nir fingers wrapped around the fabric, the white washed away and was replaced with a beautiful yellow colour, and a fiery red sun burning in the centre. Smiling slightly, ne restrung the flag, happy to not have the disgusting white hanging over nir home. When it reached the top of the pole, Trigger stepped back and observed the waving of the Team Solar flag, as something darted up to the sky behind it and exploded into a cloud of red.

Trigger jumped with shock, the boom snapping nem

out of any sense of homeland comfort as ne remembered nir situation. Running, ne continued to nir previous destination; the mayor's office; specifically the ex-ex-mayor's secret gun hidey hole, which Trigger had discovered whilst snooping in nir youth. Ne prayed that it was there, that there was still a gun inside it, that the gun still worked, and that no booby-traps had been installed in nir absence. Ne hoped for more than ne liked, given nir situation.

Inside the office was the same wooden desk, made from a single piece of wood, gifted to the first mayor of the town. Behind the old desk, under the more modern leather armchair was Trigger's target, a loose floorboard discovered by Mayor Ring, before he was replaced under President Ymany's orders. The replacement had caused much rambling amongst the public, but never enough to cause a mob to form.

Trigger burst into the office without a second-thought, and hurled the armchair across the room to get to nir prize. Pulling up the floorboard with held breath, Trigger prayed to every god ne could think of. Moving the board out of nir way, nir eyes lit up at the beautiful sight; two revolvers and a bolt-action repeating rifle. Picking them out as delicately as if they were babes, Trigger placed the guns onto the table, and checked for ammunition; rooting around underneath the floorboards, nir fingers discovered two boxes of pistol cartridges, and a pouch with twelve rifle shells inside it. As ne rose to nir feet, ne heard Kaio's voice in the distance, speaking to someone on the outskirts of the town.

Moving quickly, Trigger slipped out onto the balcony, climbed to the roof and tracked the sound to its source. Near the main town entrance, there was a thin woman watching Kaio rattle on, her brown hair pulled into a loose ponytail, showing off her elven ears; a half breed. Trigger lowered nemself onto the balcony beneath nem, and aimed at the intruder with the rifle, double checking everything ne could in silence as Kaio finished talking.

When Kaio finished, he disappeared behind one of the entrance posts, and the woman looked at her vanguard then stepped forward. Trigger fired a warning shot, and then whistled to the woman.

"The next shot won't miss," Trigger called, "Who are you? And what is this place?" The woman looked up at Trigger in surprise then raised her hands slowly.

"My name's Pandora, I'm a player, just like you. I'm on the Solar Team, I was informed that one of my teammates had captured this location, and I was looking for them... Well, I guess, I was looking for you..." Pandora swallowed, staring up at Trigger. "As for this place, your guess is as good as mine. I know that this place is called Run-Down Town, and that we're on Blue Crystal Island, but I got all that information from Kaio, who could be lying to us all..." She paused, "Who are you?"

"I'm the one with the gun," Trigger snapped, aiming it at Pandora who instantly recoiled slightly.

"Sorry, yes, you're right," Pandora blurted, moving into the shadow of the sign and finally getting a proper look at her threat; a short westerner, complete with hat, dual handguns attached to the hips and a bolt-action rifle. The unisex appearance and obvious mixture of characteristics made it impossible for Pandora to label the figure with an apparent gender or humanoid race. "Look, I want to get out of this game just as much as you, I've just come from Sun Palace, check your vanguard, how would I know that if I wasn't telling the truth?"

Breaking eye contact, Trigger twisted nir forearm and acknowledged the location she was talking about, before refocusing on nir target; however she was no longer there. Pandora stood under the balcony, breathing softly as she stared up at where Trigger was standing. Swallowing, she considered her next move, but Trigger made it for her, leaping down from the balcony. As nir feet hit the ground, Pandora made her move, spearing Trigger in the spine and tackling nem to the ground. Hitting the soil, Trigger threw nir elbow back, cracking Pandora in the face, and she reacted accordingly punching nem in the kidney.

"Get off me!" Trigger roared; reaching for the discarded rifle. Pandora grabbed nir arm, holding it still.

"Look! Look!" she shouted, holding Trigger's arm tightly, "It's the same symbol! We are on the same side!" Trigger stopped struggling as Pandora kept muttering, "We're on the same side."

***

"So, what's our next move then?" Trigger asked, sipping from nir glass of tequila. "Now that you've found me; what's our next step?" Pandora rolled her shoulders as she considered her options; they could continue towards the tower, north to the infinitely tall, shimmering tower, or head south.

"South," Pandora nodded, "Kaio's mansion is north-east, so, if we hit the location south-east, then once we have the other capture points we can pass whatever's down there."

Trigger nodded, "South it is." Ne finished nir drink and stood up, "Shall we?"

***

"Welcome warrior, to Blood Stone Maze," Kaio was wearing a respirator, that muffled his speech, "The flag for this location is in the centre of the maze, but don't breathe too deeply, the fog has different effects on different people…" The fog engulfed him, and Trigger and Pandora were left alone, staring at the entrance to the maze. From within, they could hear laughter; a mocking chuckle, and the yapping of young dogs playing wistfully, nothing felt natural about this place.

"Why is everything in this game so deadly?" Pandora asked, failing to see through the fog.

"Well, it wouldn't be entertaining if it was easy," Trigger replied, checking that nir weapons were loaded, "So, how we going to do this? Left, right or split?"

"Not split, that's a bad idea," Pandora stated quickly, fearful as to what could be hiding in the mist, "How would we regroup? I vote…" Pandora paused as she heard something yell out in a mixture of pain and anger. "…Towards that sound."

"Left it is then," Trigger replied, pulling nir goggles over nir eyes as ne took the lead. As the pair walked deeper into the labyrinth, Guffaws began to circle above them, laughing hysterically at their progress. After ten minutes of walking in the general direction of the yells, and after hitting two dead ends, Trigger finally snapped, and unloaded three kill-shots into the air, a few beats later three Guffaws hit the ground behind the blood-soaked stone walls around them.

"You didn't have to do that," Pandora began, but Trigger just raised nir hand.

"I was just adding some more blood to the maze, no harm done," ne said, filling the empty cylinders with fresh bullets. There was another yell, louder and filled with pain, the pair looked at each other briefly then hurried round the corner silently.

As they rounded the turning, they came face to face with a cute, little puppy with its large, round eyes fixed on them as its mouth opened to create an adorable smile whilst it panted. Something inside Pandora stirred, and without her consent, it rolled up her windpipe and out of her mouth;

"Nawh," Pandora smiled, before catching herself as Trigger gave her a strange sideways glance. The puppy stared up at them, licking its nostril-less nose, and after a moment of silence, the puppy let out an endearing bark, standing with its tail wagging furiously. As the pair watched it, the yell erupted once more and the pup shrank with fear, shaking at the noise that was heading towards them. Without thinking, Pandora snatched up the small animal and held it close to her.

"What are you doing?" Trigger snapped, recoiling from nir teammate, "Do you even know what that thing is?"

"No," Pandora began, before realising she didn't have an argument, "Do you?"

"No," Trigger confessed, "But that's my point. Everything in this game is deadly, remember? How do you know that isn't a trap? Like, what if it's a bomb? Did you think of that?" Pandora stared at Trigger as if ne had said the craziest thing anyone had ever said. The puppy wriggled in her arms, and propped itself up to lick her cheek.

"Nawh," Pandora said, "but it's so cute! You're not a bomb, are you? No, you're not, no, you're not." Her free hand wrapped around the pup's stomach, rubbing it. Another roar echoed down the corridor they were in, followed by stamping as a large mass threw itself down a nearby alleyway.

"Are you sure you still want us to find out what that is?" Trigger asked, aiming a revolver at the nearest corner; prepared for the worst. Pandora held the dog close to her, ready to protect the innocent animal. There was silence. A soft breeze whistled through the maze as Trigger and Pandora stared at the corner in anticipation, their heartbeats racing in fear and excitement. Suddenly there was movement to Trigger's left, and a feminine scream, as the small dog's mouth enlarged and it sunk its teeth into Pandora's shoulder. As Trigger turned, a large figure smashed into the wall across from the corner they had been watching, eight small shadows nipping at its heels.

Something clicked in Trigger's mind, and nir eyes glazed as nir targets were highlighted, and nir brain figured out the best method of elimination in a matter of nanoseconds. Without a second's pause, Trigger unholstered nir other revolver and fired five shots. Nine bodies hit the ground, and then Pandora fell to her knees and held her shoulder. The figure stood in shock, and then began to advance, Trigger stepped between the darkened shape and nir teammate. It was hard to make out any details, but Trigger could see that it had a muscular body, and a horned head.

"Hold it right there, mister," Trigger said, aiming

both revolvers at the final, potential threat.

"I only want to help, miss," It had a soft, cowardly, yet deep voice, but Trigger didn't lower nir guard.

"Not a 'miss'. Who are you?" ne demanded.

"Sorry, I'm…" the figure began, before falling silent as the yapping of nearby dogs floated towards them. Fear coated his voice as he asked, "Do you know a way out, sir?"

"We're not leaving until we find the flag, and if you call me a 'sir' again, I'll blow your horns off," Trigger threatened, before turning nir head slightly and whispering; "You alright, Panny?" Pandora nodded, grunting a response of yes.

"The flag? I, I know where it is, the white flag in the fog, it's back that way. I could, I could take you to it? Then you could get us out, right?" the figure began to fidget, the barks growing in volume as they came to investigate the gunshots.

"Panny?" Trigger asked, whilst staring at the twitchy shadow.

"We need to move, I don't think I'd be much use in a fight right now…" Pandora answered quietly.

"Deal. Lead the way, but if you try anything, I'll bury a bullet between your eyes, understand?" Trigger questioned.

"Completely, come on, they're nearly here, and the birds, the birds work with them, and then we'll never escape," the figure answered, beginning to move back the way he came, Trigger followed quickly keeping them both within nir sights, whilst Pandora stumbled behind, gripping her shoulder tightly. The trio moved in silence, cautious of any noises by potential threats, after a confusing hour of turns, they found themselves in the centre of the maze.

A metal flagpole stood proudly in the centre of the clearing, protruding out of a lit fire pit. The white, uncaptured flag hung riskily close to the blazes outstretched reach, mocking the flames. Opposite the trio, the northern entrance stood unguarded, Trigger sped around the pit and glanced down the corridor.

"Touch the flag," Trigger demanded, quickly returning and checking Pandora's shoulder.

"What?" he asked, "Why would I? It could be poisonous."

"It's not poisonous," Pandora reassured, blood soaking into her top again as Trigger pulled it loose from her wound, "We're not the bad guys, okay? We want to get out of here just as much as you do, trust us." The figure, stared at them shaking, then stepped forward, and stretched out a trembling hand over the flames, toward the flag. As his finger touched it, the white was replaced with the comforting yellow and red which Pandora and Trigger now knew. Trigger glanced over at the flag, down at Pandora and then to their new teammate.

"Great. Now, pick up Pandora and let's get out of here," Trigger demanded. Ne had moved to the southern entrance when ne spotted a murder of Guffaws hanging overhead, and was met with the sight of distant shadows convulsing with canine movement.

"What? Pick up? Her? Why would I...?" the man stumbled.

"Enough questions! Do it, now!" Trigger shouted as the shadows twisted violently as more of the dogs joined the chase towards them. "Move!" Hastily, the horned man picked up Pandora as if she were a doll, and dashed through the northern doorway, Trigger chasing after them. When they passed three dead Guffaws and Trigger's discarded shells, ne passed Pandora and the horned man, and they rushed through the final stretch of the labyrinth, twisting and turning towards the hopeful exit, that Trigger prayed ne remembered. The dogs were fast on their heels, barking viciously in the fog. Trigger seemed to release a barrage of bullets at every turning, attempting to keep the dogs at bay, whilst the horned man never slowed, in fear of being caught by the mutts again.

After another hour of running, the trio burst out of the maze, the fresh air wrapping around them in its clear, cooling grip. In the new lighting, Trigger turned to see that Pandora was being held in the arms of a muscular Minotaur. The Minotaur inhaled deeply, spun on the spot, faced the entrance confidently, and then covering Pandora with his free arm, he breathed out a fiery blast, setting the dogs ablaze.

"Die you fucking animals!" The Minotaur roared, breathing deeply, before muttering, "I've always hated Hush Curs..." The Minotaur then put Pandora down and turned to face Trigger, "Thank you, friend, allow me to introduce myself properly; I am Oxar." Trigger stared silently in surprise at Oxar's courageous feat, and fearless voice in contrast to the beast they had known moments before, before nodding and replying;

"Trigger," ne pointed at nemself, then at Pandora, "Pandora. We are your Solar teammates."

Oxar nodded,

"Then I suppose we are family now."

Trigger and Pandora looked at one another, and then nodded in response.

Pandora rolled her slowly healing shoulder,

"Let's get back to Run-Down and rest up."

Chapter Nine
Steel Skinned Spy

01010010 00110001 01010110 00111001 00100000
01110000 01110010 01101111 01100111 01110010
01100001 01101101 00100000 01100001 01100011
01110100 01101001 01110110 01100001 01110100
01100101 01100100

>$ perl –E 'say 01010010 00111001 01110110 00111001'
>"82 49 118 57"
>$ perl –E 'say chr(82 49 118 57)'
>"R1v9"

>Installation complete

R9's eyes lit up red as its programming activated, its positronic brain booting up as Professor's variation of the robotic laws were uploaded. Mechanical arms lifted R9's head and fixed it onto the advanced robotics body that had followed Professor's latest blue prints. Programs initiated analysing the new connections and motion capabilities. The mechanical arms lifted R9 off of the table and placed it onto the nearby conveyer belt, behind R8 and R7, before proceeding to shut down.

The pressure pad under the conveyer belt activated, triggering the belt to switch on. R9 and its electronic brethren slid forward, triggering analytics software to check the robots for faults. As R9 stared blankly forwards, R7 was torn in half by two powerful magnets on either side of the belt. The belt turned a corner, as wires latched onto the two remaining robots, switching on their movement relays, their internal power supplies and encoding Professor's DNA onto their hands. Images flashed into R9's mind, instructing it to move in different ways to diagnose its movement abilities.

After moving its body, R9 was commanded to move into the central room of the building it was stood in. As it moved, it observed its surroundings; an old observatory repurposed by its creator to act as her temporary laboratory. R9 stood in a small squad of six other R-units, all branded with an R and a number on their left chest plate and right shoulder. R9's vision scanned the other units: 2, 4, 5, 6, and 8, whilst R3 stood in front of the squad, next to their creator: Professor.

Professor stood monitoring the squad in front of her, new designs spawning in her brain on how to make the next model of units better than the ones in front of her. She wore glasses with black rims, and her blonde hair was in a high ponytail, exposing her pointed elven ears, she was also sporting a green shirt with black trousers under a stained laboratory coat, which was burnt along the sleeve edges. The light reflected off of her glasses as her eyes locked onto R9, it could feel its circuitry limit itself as certain functions were switched off; a failsafe to prevent any of the deadly automatons attacking her.

"R-units!" she shouted, "Your primary purpose is

surveillance, and to capture the flags using my DNA, once receiving the confirmation message. Your secondary objective is to kill the members of the opposing team, identifiable by the sun logo on their arms." It was at this moment, Professor pointed up at the ceiling where the Nocturnal flag hung between opposing paintings of a moon and a sun.

"Using the map of the island I have uploaded into your memory banks, you will travel to those capture points and, when given the order, capture those flags in one quickened swoop to grant me victory." Professor announced to room, re-confirming the information programmed in the R-units brains, this was more for herself than for her robotic soldiers, "R2, you will go north to Nocturnal Castle and War Forest and seek out my two living teammates. R3, you will reside here as my security whilst I upgrade my weaponry. R4, 5, 6, 8 and 9, you will go to your designated capture points and await orders. Confirm!"

The squad opened the salute file, and all announced; "Huzzah!"

***

R9 ran until it reached its target; central east of the island, as it slowed, R6 sped off southward. R9 leapt over the wooden fence that surrounded the timber town, and then, enabling the sensors in its fingertips, climbed the flat building side. Upon reaching the top, its audio sensors detected speaking in the centre of the town. As R9 approached, it spotted the pallid flag hanging on a flagpole in the civic midpoint. Casting its sights across the clearing, R9 acknowledged three figures sat around a small camp fire. Its optics targeted the trio and adjusted to the dim lighting; a human-elf, a Minotaur and another humanoid.

As its audio sensors focused on the trio, R9 heard the humanoid whisper to the human-elf.

"We're being watched," ne said, "Don't make any sudden movements." R9 surveyed the area, trying to find another source for this statement, as it had monitored its own movements and remained invisible to human perceptions. As this electronic signal was created, a rifle bullet smashed into R9's chest, sending it off the rooftop. Impacting with the ground, its power supply was knocked out of place and the R-unit shutdown.

***

Oxar and Pandora stood over the robotic man that Trigger had blown off the roof, the only thing that had ever been able to sneak up on Pandora. It was mostly humanoid in appearance, with smooth metallic skin, yet the round speaker inside a square mouth gap and the wide-open black optics, stopped anyone mistaking it for a humanoid covered in silver paint.

"Is this another player?" Oxar enquired, crouching next to the body.

"My guess is no," Pandora answered, rubbing her shoulder and testing how well the wound had healed. Oxar frowned up at her, so she continued with her reasoning; "It doesn't have one of these stupid vanguards..."

"Could have figured out a way of taking it off...?" Oxar replied.

"It's not a player!" Trigger shouted from the

campfire, reloading nir rifle, "From what I've seen on TV, Kaio only chooses humanoid players, things that can die and feel bad about killing."

"Then what is it doing here?" Oxar asked after a pause, "Another player make it?"

"Maybe," Pandora answered, "Trigger found guns, who know what else is hidden on this island…?" The distant Guffaws began chuckling again, before venturing to Blood Stone Maze, Trigger and Pandora hadn't been able to hear them, but now that they knew the birds were there, the laughter seemed to cover the distance unaffectedly.

"So, what are we going to do with it?" Trigger asked, poking the fire.

"Could have a tracking device inside," Pandora began, "We could take it apart and see what makes it tick, get an idea of what we're up against." Pandora's proposal got a silent response, which she took as a yes.

"Oxar, could you disconnect the external chest panel?" Pandora asked, getting herself comfortable, with enough light from the flames to see what she was about to do.

"Once more in Vanicrasian?" Oxar replied, the request flying over his head.

Pandora sighed, responding, "Could you take off the front of its chest?" Pandora said, over pronouncing each word as if speaking to a child. She got the reaction she desired, as Oxar huffed and pulled a face, before tearing off the robot's chest plate, "Thank you, Oxar. I'll call if I need you for anything else."

Oxar rolled his eyes and returned to the fire, laying down on one of the mattresses they had dragged out of the nearby houses. Pandora watched him go, and then focused on the job at hand. She had a fairly strong love for technology, and it had come in great use whilst on contracts whereby the intended object was locked away behind electronic security systems. Tipping the robot towards the fire to cast more light inside, Pandora realised that the knowledge she'd gained was vastly inferior for her desired project, but this didn't halt her progress.

After isolating the power supply, and removing the bullet from a damaged matrix board, Pandora realised that she had focused on the wrong part of the android. Moving around the steel corpse, Pandora propped its head up on a rock and proceeded to feel the mechanized cranium until she found a button just above its nape. Pressing the button, part of the shell slid upwards and, Pandora could see its positronic brain with its deceivingly complex appearance, however after looking at it for a few moments, Pandora realised that it was no more complex than the robotic doll her father had given her as a girl. Licking her fingertips, she dove in the electronic mayhem, where one slip could change this silent spy into a giant paperweight. As she connected the main software drive to an internal screen, Pandora got to work.

Oxar was snoring by the time she'd finished tinkering inside the robot's head, Trigger, however, was still staring into the flames, nir brain ticking away, dwelling on nir past.

"Trigger," Pandora whispered, snapping nem out of nir trance, Trigger looked over. "I'm turning it on, be ready in case I've made a mistake." Ne nodded, grabbing nir rifle. Pandora swallowed, closing R9's skull and reaching into its chest cavity to reconnect its power supply.

>01000101 01110010 01110010 01101111 01110010
>Error
>"R1v9" unavailable
>Opening "P.F.R9" program
>Boot up sequence activated

R9's eyes lit up an emerald green as it stared up at the night sky, the stars twinkling above it. System diagnostics informed it that it was fine, but its memory bank informed it that much had changed; its objectives had been wiped clean and it was no longer bound to Professor's variation of the robotic laws. R9 sat up slowly, and observed its surroundings: a sleeping Minotaur, an individual pointing a gun at R9 and a woman knelt beside it. R9 stared at this woman the longest, new data activating in its system.

"Pandora," R9 announced, "You are the one that broke my programming. Confirm?" The woman nodded in reply.

"My internal network diagnosis informs me that you have... Why?" R9 asked, its electronic voice loud enough for Trigger to hear too, but not noisy enough to wake the slumbering Minotaur.

"Because, it's better to turn an opponent into a friend, than into a dead opponent," Pandora answered.

"A friend?" asked R9, its processors working quickly to process this information, as it looked forwards. Pandora reattached R9's chest plate, "What is it that you want from me?"

"What do you want?" Pandora asked in response, smiling as this question confused the robot.

"I was created specifically to kill you, and capture your flag, so that you would lose…" R9 began, "Without a designated objective… I still desire to win *Eclipse*. As my thanks, I will join your team to achieve this goal." R9 looked at Pandora, "Better to keep your ex-enemies close." Pandora smirked.

"Wonderful," Trigger called, lowering nir weapon, "Another questionable ally in this stupid game. Any more great ideas, Panny?"

Pandora stood up and walked over to the flames,

"We need to meet our opponents, see what we're up against…"

"I can be of assistance there," R9 pitched in, "Team Nocturnal are planning to travel to the tower at the centre of the island, after meeting at Dreamer's Observatory."

Trigger and Pandora nodded.

"The tower it is," Pandora said, staring into the flames.

Trigger covered nemself with a scavenged blanket, before throwing another at Pandora.

Oxar snored calmly, his wounds from the maze healing in the night air.

R9 lay back down to observe the stars, letting its mind generate insane visuals, experiencing what it believed to be 'dreams'.

Chapter Ten
Nocturnal Commercial Break

The grand stage lit up to reveal Kaio, stood centre stage wearing his trademark red and black suit, a tall black top hat, with red lace, whilst holding a black cane with a red handle. An electronic audience applauded as the room illuminated, Kaio tipped his hat and smiled widely.

"Hello Ladies and Gentlemen, and welcome back to *Eclipse*, the daily programme broadcasted and hosted by yours truly. Now, before the main event, I've created a few short adverts based on the backgrounds of some of our favourite players. So, without more time wasting; here's what I've come up with…" Kaio tapped the cane on the ground and the lights blacked out.

***

When the lights returned, the stage had been made up like a study, complete with a messy desk, a full bookcase and a brown leather-backed chair and, down-stage right stood a young warlock boy, staring out at the audience, with eyes begging for help. The boy sniffed and wiped his cheek, a bottle smashed offstage causing the boy to jump and run to hide behind the small leather-backed armchair.

"Hello there, little warlock," Kaio's disembodied voice spoke softly, "Is your father home?" The boy nodded, quickly, his eyes fixed on the door beside the bookcase.

"Well, I imagine you'd like to go give your old man a hug?" The boy shook his head furiously at Kaio's question, "Well, perhaps you'd prefer to take revenge? Become the new man of the house? How does that sound?" The boy stood slowly, thinking before nodding as he came out of his hiding spot, and took centre stage, a spotlight tracking the young warlock.

"Well, you're in luck little warlock, because Yanstag's Mana Academy are always on the lookout for new students willing to study the difficult arts of magic. For the cheap, cheap price of lifetime loyalty, you can learn how to break the universe to your will, and how you shouldn't do any of the crazy, dangerous, fun spells you will read about. Sound good to you?" Kaio asked, as the boy's expression changed from excitement, to confusion, to mischief, then he nodded in response, smiling.

"Excellent! Join Yanstag's Mana Academy, applications accepted all year round! We hope to see you very soon, so long as you promise to not experiment in Dark Magic, or allow ambition to cloud your path to be an observer of the Vanicrast ways. Promise?" The boy hid his hand behind his back, before nodding, smiling sweetly.

"Wonderful!" Kaio shouted, "We look forward to your application!" As the stage fell silent, the boy looked forward at the audience before checking the coast was clear, and then the boy brought his hand from behind his back revealing cross-keys. The artificial audience laughed loudly as the lights faded.

***

When the lights relit, the stage had been transformed into a giant bird's nest, a female harkall wearing a black cloak sat in the centre.

"Has this ever happened to you?" Kaio's disembodied voice asked rhetorically, before continuing, "You're just sat considering life, when suddenly it dawns on you; you could be a better leader than the royals that are currently doing a terrible job! Well, we have just the product for you, introducing; 'Rebellion in a Bag'." As Kaio announced a small bag landed in the harkall's lap, "For the small price of an eighth Kaio coin or a single gold bar, you can make all your wildest rebellion dreams come true." The harkall opened the bag, and pulled out a pack of permanent markers, some customisable arm bands, and a knife.

"Yes, all the pain of resource gathering, has been done for you, so that all you need to do is grab a few comrades, come up with the name and what you stand for, and away you'll be. With 'Rebellion in a Bag', you can kick off changing the world in a matter of hours. To demonstrate the effectiveness of our product, we've had a harkall create a rebellious group whilst we've been talking." The harkall lifted an A1 piece of card which said; 'Replace the Royals' with a red dove underneath it.

"In just a matter of minutes, this woman has gone from being a nobody to becoming the leader of a rebellious organisation known as the 'Murder of Doves', with dreams of replacing the lazy monarchs that have eaten the profits of the land of Harkall. What will you do with this product? Call this number now." A fake number flashed above the stage for a few moments before another black out.

***

The stage was reset to present a doctor's office; a sickly woman was sat in front of the empty desk as soft music clicked on.

"They were there when you were born, they will be there when you die, but in recent years, the inability to produce enough blood cells has become an unfortunately common occurrence. Well, for a small donation of your life, you can be subjected to experimental tests with the possibility of curing your disease." Kaio announced, as the woman began to become healthier. "And with a 0.001% chance of being an improbable monster with the insane ability of limited shape shifting, what do you really have to lose? So! Donate now, and receive excellent health care and the chance of a cure; you're going to die anyway…" The soft music played on as the woman got up and walked off the stage happily, the lights dimming as she walked.

***

"With Winter just round the bend, are you prepared for the icy weather, the sweat freezing winds or the constant state of wetness? If you answered no to any of these questions, then you're in luck," The lights flicked on revealing Kaio in a fictional representation of Zxaperia, complete with fire and comically small demons with pitchforks, "Zxaperia contains such beautiful sights and sounds as the relaxing Nightmare Plains, the musical Torture Isles and the legendary Frozen Blood River, where you can even meet Lord Termin in the flesh! And all of this can be yours for the cheap, cheap price of your soul! Finally, it's good for something!" Kaio smiled, "You'll love it so much that the only way we'll be able to get you out is if we throw you out of a summoner's mouth!" A soft chanting began through the speakers.

"Speak of the Termin, sounds like my ride's here, but you can bet I'll be back soon enough!" Black out.

***

"Coming to a television near you," Kaio announced in the darkness, "Last season, we watched Dystopia's infamous child snatcher, Snatcher, fight it out in *Eclipse*. Now, watch as one of those kids plays for themselves!" Suddenly, all the lights were turned on at once, temporarily blinding any of unprepared viewers of the broadcast. Onstage was a woman in a dirty lab coat holding a large, mechanical gun aimed at killer robots and holographic monster, they all stood in motionless action poses. "The elf born in Vilderton, has been selected to fight in *Eclipse*! Reviewers are calling it, the best thing since season sixteen! Some people are even asking how it hadn't happened earlier! But this season; watch as one female player, stands up for what she believes in and fights a battle against time, space and death itself! *Eclipse*! Season seventeen! Broadcasting right now!"

Chapter Eleven
Nocturnal Meeting

The sun had set by the time Gronix and Murados arrived at Dreamer's Observatory, following the robotic unit. Whilst travelling through the dangerous terrain, they had both told one another a version of their past; Gronix the wrongfully-expelled warlock, and Murados the result of experimental surgery. In front of them was the tapering of the valley that diagonally crossed the island from south-west to north-northwest. The trio slipped between two large hills, where the ground was only a few inches below surface level, and the landscape revealed their destination; a large, abandoned observatory that had fallen to severe disrepair. As they stepped up onto the other side of the small dip, Kaio's holographic program activated. Gronix and Murados stopped in front of Kaio, whilst the android continued into the observatory.

"Welcome Warrior, to Dreamer's Observatory." Kaio stood wearing an immaculate lab coat, complete with pens in the pocket. "The flag for this location is on the ceiling inside the telescope room of the observatory. Whilst you're there, don't forget to look through the telescope and remember just how small you really are." At the end of his monologue, Omiss phased up from the ground beneath him, as Kaio exploded into stardust.

"What did you find?" Gronix asked, un-phased by Omiss's entrance.

"An elf and more robots," Omiss answered; his words elongated and sinister, his eyes wondered across the scene in front of him before landing upon Murados, whose flesh crawled at the sight of him.

"Level of threat?" Gronix asked, advancing towards the observatory entrance.

"Minimum," Omiss stated, before continuing quietly to Murados, "for me." His mouth cracked into a cruel smile, before he turned and followed his summoner.

Murados shivered, the sight of Omiss triggered temporary nightmares from her time in Zxaperia, the earliest memories she still had. Flashes of torture and pain, mentally and spiritually torn apart whilst her Vanicrast bound corpse was experimented on further by the scientists who had murdered her. Her skin rippled as her mind flicked through the images captured in her brain; pictures of Zxaperia, the photographs of her first kill that had become third person from over thinking, and freeze frames of each kill since.

"Are you coming?" Gronix called, stood by the door as Omiss phased through it. Murados didn't reply, choosing instead to let her actions speak for themselves as her five legs raced to the door with effortless haste. As she got close, Gronix opened the door wide, "Arachne-women first." His two-faced smile wasn't acknowledged as Murados entered the unknown first.

"Murados! Or would you prefer Miranda Sty?" Professor shouted down from an elevated level as her two teammates entered the main room of the observatory, standing beside another robotic man: R3.

"Why would you call me that?" Murados responded bitterly, looking around the room as her legs tapped the ground.

"Well, the most obvious reason, would be because it's your name..." Professor replied, putting down a small screwdriver. Gronix came into view as Murados moved further in. "And Gronix Void! The infamous dark warlock of Yanstag."

"What do you mean that's my name?" Murados demanded.

"Welcome to Dreamer's Observatory!" Professor roared, ignoring Murados's question. "It's still a long way from being a shadow of my laboratory back in Haula, but it's sufficient for our purposes," she continued, climbing down the spiral staircase, the robots following her closely.

"Nice place," Gronix stated, glancing at the electronic wonder they had entered. Professor had recycled all the supplies that had been left in the building to create a compact robot factory, a large screen with access to the online landscape outside of Blue Crystal Island, and an assortment of weaponry that lay on tables around the space.

"And," Professor began as she reached the bottom of the steps, waiting until she had them both in full view before continuing, "I am Professor." She stood proudly, and Murados kept her eyes trained on her as she seemed to hold important information to her past, whilst Gronix had spotted a monitor with nine screens; seven showing footage and two blank. On two of the live screens, he could see himself and Murados, helping him deduce that the monitors were electronically connected to the robots' eyes.

"Professor what?" Gronix asked, half paying attention as he watched one of the screens pan onto three other players before going black.

"What?" Professor asked in reply, momentarily confused, "Oh, no. My name is, Professor, I'm from Dystopia…" She stared at the blank faces, then nodded and instead continued, "I was named in a time period, where your title and your name are the same thing."

"Why did you say my name was Miranda?" Murados asked, growing angry at the obvious disregard for her questions on a subject that was of high importance to her.

"Because it *is* your name…" Professor replied plainly, before looking at Murados as the penny dropped, "You don't remember, do you?"

"Can you rewind these visuals?" Gronix interrupted as another screen went black.

"What?" Professor replied, her attention snapping to him, "Yes, of course, I designed it to have a twenty-four hour memory file. That way, if anything happened to one of the units, I could…"

"Rewind these two." Gronix demanded, pointing at the fourth and ninth screen on the monitor.

"Excuse me," Professor snapped, "I don't remember you becoming the leader of this little group, so if you wouldn't mind showing a little respect."

"What do you know about my past?" Murados screamed as her patience shattered. Professor spun to face her, as Murados approached.

"You best calm down girl! I am not afraid to destroy an anomaly!" Professor ordered, her hand shooting into the air. As it did, R2 and R3 picked up two of the weapons that Professor had created and aimed them at the furious life-form that appeared arachne. Feeling threatened, something inside her Orákon-tainted blood snapped awake, and in the blink of an eye, Murados was on top of the closest threat; R2. Her claws tore through the robot's chest plate, before her head snapped back and she spat webbing at the R3 unit, forcing it against one of the balcony supports. Professor grabbed one of her weapons from a nearby table and aimed it at Murados.

Stillness. Gronix had turned to face his teammates, and was disgusted to witness these violent acts, that would only weaken his position in his attempt to win. Raising his hands, Gronix's eyes blurred black, as both Murados and Professor stopped moving, their blood slowing, their muscles tensing to the point of pain. They both began to scream in agony as their bodies began to collapse beneath them.

"I will not stand for this unruly behaviour! I am your commander! I am your leader! And you will obey my commands, so that we can triumph! Understood?" Gronix roared, tightening his grip on their bodies after each sentence. Following an age of screaming, the two finally managed to utter the word 'yes', and once the utterance had reached Gronix's ears, he released them.

"Now, Professor, rewind these two," he repeated, spitting out her name with the same level of respect as with a disobedient child, pointing at the previous screens. Nodding, Professor rose slowly and stumbled to the computer, holding her stomach tightly as her sore muscles argued with every minor movement she made. With a few clicks, both screens were back to the point, a few moments, before they lost connection.

The ninth screen showed three figures: a large Minotaur and two smaller, undistinguishable humanoids, sat around a small fire.

"We're being watched," one of the figures said, "Don't make any sudden movements." The screen panned the surroundings quickly, showing a small wooden town similar to the ones Gronix read about whilst studying 'Riodic's History of Mana Shifts'. Then without warning the screen snapped back, the footage panning backwards from the sky as the unit fell to the ground below, and then the visuals went blank.

Team Nocturnal stared at the footage, Gronix rubbed his chin before nodding.

"Team Solar," He stated, still staring at the blank screen, "This could be an easy challenge after all." He smiled, and then indicated for Professor to start the fourth screen.

Pressing the play button, the trio were staring at a tall, thick, stone tower, similar to one that may be spoken in the same breath as a princess and a dragon. The screen stealthily made its way around the tower before arriving at a pair of unnecessarily large, wooden doors, with words carved onto the front panels, but the screen's constant movement made it impossible for them to make out. Arriving in front of the doors, the screen checked its surroundings then snuck into the building.

It was dark, but the flickering of a distant fire helped the screen adjust to the sudden lighting change. It began its standing scan of the room, panning slowly from the left wall. However, it had not covered twenty degrees before a large, bony hand appeared engulfing the image. The shadow held the screen for a few moments before it was disconnected.

Professor sighed as she realised that her designs needed a lot more work if they were to survive this vicious place.

"Where did the footage come from?" Gronix asked, staring at the blank screens.

"R9 had arrived in the central-east of the island, whilst R4 was broadcasting from the centre." Professor replied, rubbing her aching sides, as she nodded at each screen respectively.

"Then that's where we'll go," Gronix answered, "and I bet Solar team will be doing the same, especially if you inform your R-units of that information."

"Why would I do that?" Professor enquired, frowning slightly.

"Because, if your 'R9' is still able to receive our messages, there may be a chance that the Solar Team will use it to determine our movements," Gronix responded, assuming that his plan was both genius and obvious.

Professor nodded, typing into the computer.

Murados watched her closely, waiting for her moment to interrogate Professor about her knowledge about 'Miranda Sty'.

Gronix stared at the monitor, and smirked.

Whilst, Omiss drummed his nails against his teeth, waiting impatiently for the mortal to give him permission, to cause beautiful, nightmarish chaos.

Chapter Twelve
Central Tower

Team Solar woke to peaceful silence, and a juicy meat scent climbing up their nostrils. Pandora was the first to brave the reality of their situation, expecting the peace to disperse as quickly as the scent, but as she rose to a seated position, neither evaporated, instead the smell grew, the aroma swirling down her nasal cavity into her mouth and attempting to drown her in saliva. Opening her eyes, she was momentarily blinded by the sun rise and the smoke that surrounded their little camp. Pandora waved her hand, turning her face for a beat, before looking again and seeing R9 plating up a cooked Guffaw onto three flat rocks.

"Good morning," R9 said, without looking at her, "I have prepared breakfast, so that we may leave with haste." Finally, it turned to her and presented her with the meal.

"Erm, thanks," Pandora said, unsurely taking the plate and staring at it suspiciously.

"I understand your suspicion," R9 stated, its optical processors tracking her facial expressions whilst it was facing her general direction, "If it puts you at ease, I recorded two hundred and fifty three ways I could have killed you whilst you slept, and as I do not have full control over the new coding you entered into my system, I would not have felt too bad about doing it." Pandora watched R9 simultaneously fearful and eased.

"Food poisoning, however, would only be seen as a fault in my programming. This would cause my internal diagnoses' to shut down, effectively ending my new consciousness," R9 finished. It then looked directly at her face adding, "Also, I intend to understand the true extent of what you have given me. Confirm?"

Pandora stared at R9, whilst its words sank into her mind. Pandora's brain picked apart R9's argument and concluded that it was saying; why would I kill you, after you freed me?

"Confirmed," Pandora stated, smiling a little as she bit into the cooked poultry.

"You may want to pull in your left leg," R9 recommended, turning back to the food.

"Why?" Pandora quizzed, cautiously pulling her left leg under her right. Oxar's actions answered her question, as he woke and sprinted into the town, his right foot smashing the earth where her leg had been seconds before.

"Because, the Minotaur has a full bladder," R9 stated, plating up the second plate and presenting it to Trigger, who was laying still with nir hat covering nir eyes.

"I think Trigger's still asleep," Pandora said, taking another bite.

"Incorrect," R9 declared, holding still, "I have been monitoring all three of your vitals since returning with your food. Results conclude that the subject, Trigger, has been awake for one hour, but did not want to risk being attacked first, so continued to act asleep until another risked themselves." Trigger's mouth twitched beneath nir hat.

"You, little…" Pandora began, her smile widening. Trigger let out a small laugh as ne pushed nir hat back with one finger.

"You're a clever little robot, huh?" Trigger chuckled.

"Affirmative," R9 stated, as Trigger took the plate from its fingers, and it turned to plate up the last of the meat. Oxar strolled back to camp, relieved.

"So, you got it working then," Oxar asked as his eyes acknowledged the steel chef that had prepared the group food, that the other two were happily feasting upon.

"Could, 'it' be referred to as 'R9'?" R9 asked, presenting Oxar with his plate of food.

"You can be referred to as 'My lord' if you keep cooking me grub," Oxar chuckled, as the meat smells wafted up his nostrils. Licking his lips, Oxar took the food and sat on the mattress he had slept on, while R9 began tidying up its mess. Oxar devoured his meal quickly, before looking over at the other two, who had not yet reached the halfway point of theirs. Wiping his mouth, he asked, "So, what's the plan now, team?"

"We're going to that big tower to the west," Trigger stated, with a mouthful of meat, "That's where the other team's heading too, so if we get there first, we can capture the flag and be in a better position when we finally all come face to face."

"Face-to-face?" Oxar repeated, "So, you're expecting a fight?" Silence fell over the camp as Pandora and Trigger looked at Oxar.

"You haven't seen a lot of these games before, have you?" Pandora asked, praying that she wouldn't have to clarify the terms of the 'game' they were subject to.

"Not really," Oxar confessed, "I've not really spent a lot of time around televisions... or people outside my family..."

"Nope!" Trigger shouted, rising to nir feet. "That sounds like a whole can of worms that I have no intention of opening." Ne turned to Oxar and continued, "When we meet the other team, there will be fighting, and just like with the Hush Curs, things will die. Us or them. Them's the rules. Now, I'm gonna go take a piss, come back, gather my stuff, and then we're going to march on up to death's door and give it a knock. Okay?" Trigger didn't wait for an answer, instead turning on nir heels and striding off to a nearby house to use its toilet. Oxar and Pandora sat in silence for a moment, R9's activities providing the only audible noise as they waited for the other to speak first.

"Look, what Trigger meant was..." Pandora began, but Oxar cut her off.

"No, it is fine, I understand. When I was in the fog, some guy told me that we were playing a game of capture the flag and that if we die, we'd respawn at our headquarters..." Oxar said softly, "I just never connected that I might die from somebody killing me... Fun game, huh?"

Pandora sighed, nodded, and then replied with a weak, "Yeah, a real hoot."

***

Team Solar arrived at the front of the gigantic stone tower at noon, making it impossible for them to look up at the buildings impressive height without being blinded by the sun's rays.

"This building stands at 500.2 metres high, with an estimated floor area of 190,800m^2," R9 stated, its mind using the terrain and observable distance to calculate this information.

"Does he realise that means nothing to us?" Oxar asked Pandora, who was busy trying to make out the words carved onto the massive wooden doors in front of them.

"Speak for yourself," Trigger said, aiming nir rifle at a distant target, before lowering it once ne realised that it was just a Wobok hunting berries.

"What does the writing say, R9?" Pandora enquired, her eyes struggling to make out the rotten words that had been damaged by time, weather and players past. R9's eyes cast a green light upon the door, scanning the lines slowly before correcting the words with holographic, emerald letters.

Welcome Warriors, to Central Tower,
The flag for this location is at the very peak of the skyscraper.
Inside you will find my son, CHAMP.
I would ask you to play nice,
But I know he won't...
Have Fun!

"I'd thought it was strange that there hadn't been another one of Kaio's holograms recently," Pandora said, reading his message aloud.

"What sort of person names their child Champ?" Oxar asked.

"The same sort of person that would lock their kid in

a tower on the middle of death-trap island," Trigger replied, nir attention darting to the horizon before relaxing again. The emerald writing flickered then disappeared.

"Actually, my scan indicates that the door is open," R9 stated, moving to the entrance, "Shall we proceed?" R9 pulled the door open with an audible creak.

"Well, there goes the element of surprise…" Trigger sighed. Then the three stepped into the darkened tower in unison, R9 following them and shutting the door.

A fire flickered on the far side of the room, on the other side of a grand spiral staircase that seemed to climb up to the heavens. Trigger led the way, rifle ready, with nir finger on the trigger, Pandora followed close; holding sharpened stones as knives as she moved silently, Oxar's footsteps echoed off the walls no matter how hard he tried, whilst R9 had activated a softening agent in the balls of his feet to cushion his movements.

"Where do you think this 'Champ' is?" Oxar whispered.

"Shut up," Trigger replied quietly, aiming at the shadows dancing on the walls.

"Do you think he's even in here?" Oxar asked, the bass quality of his voice betraying his attempt to speak softly.

"Speak again, and I will shoot you," Trigger reasoned, nir words barely reaching the Minotaur.

Pandora began counting her breaths, her notion of time dissolving as they edged across the room, she had experienced similar situations whilst out on contracts, but never without the element of surprise; she felt vulnerable to whatever was hiding in the dark. Her eyes scanned the darkness making out the outlines of chairs, tables, and a mixture of complete and broken bookshelves. As the group reached the grand spiral staircase in the middle of the room, they began to hear a soft whistling that slowly grew in volume. Pandora swallowed as Trigger pressed nemself against the staircase and began edging round.

On the other side of the staircase were six bentwood chairs seated around a small fire, a steaming kettle hanging above the flames. In the furthest chair, staring at them was a tall, skeleton-thin man with grey hair and wings, wearing a waistcoat and jeans.

"Sit," the stranger demanded, taking the pot off of the heat and pouring the content into four cups. The group froze, their eyes darting around the room for another person, but when their gaze fell on the stranger again, he was smiling at them, "I won't ask again."

R9 made the first move, strolling forward past its team, and sitting in the closest chair as requested. The flames reflected in the stranger's eyes as he watched the robot advance, his smile never moving.

"I assume you don't want any Whystar," the stranger stated, "Due to your inability to consume it." R9 nodded, watching the stranger's movements unblinkingly. After a few moments of silence, Trigger advanced, rifle lowered but ready to lock onto the stranger in a heartbeat. Trigger sat to R9's left, placing the rifle on nir lap, nir hand still wrapped around the handle. The moment ne was seated; Oxar stomped to the seat on R9's right, falling into the chair carelessly. Pandora surveyed her options before moving; between the stranger and Oxar, or between Trigger and the stranger. Tightening her grip on her makeshift daggers, Pandora moved gracefully to sit next to Trigger.

"Thank you," the stranger said, looking around the circle, "I hate having to kill intruders before introductions." With that he passed Pandora a cup of Whystar and indicated for her to pass it round before passing her another two cups. Once the four cups had been delivered to the four people who could drink the hot, sweet-smelling liquid, the stranger raised his cup giving a silent 'cheers' as he made eye contact with each of his unwelcome guests, and then he sipped the content.

From this distance, Pandora was able to distinguish more of the stranger's features; the stubble that was scattered unevenly across his chin, the way his featherless wings were burnt with the skin tightly clinging to the bones beneath the surface and the facial similarities to their captor; Kaio.

"You're Champ, aren't you?" Pandora asked when he had lowered his cup.

"What gave it away?" he replied, "The way my name was written on the door? Or was it my inherited good-looks?" Champ smirked,

"Yes, I am Champ. Kaio's created 'son', a wondrous step forward in both science and magic. While you are; Pandora, Trigger, R-unit-9 and Oxar," Champ stated, pointing at each of them respectively, "And you are here to capture the flag upstairs." Champ sipped his drink once more.

"And you're going to let us?" Oxar asked; his voice sprinkled with hope. Champ spluttered into his cup, before pulling it away from his mouth and laughing loudly, the laughter echoed off the stone walls.

"Let you? HA! Oh, you are funny!" Champ roared between chuckles, before winking at Oxar and saying, "I'll kill you last." He continued to snicker to himself as he finished off his drink.

Trigger put nir untouched beverage on the ground slowly, and placed both nir hands on nir rifle. R9's internal sensors acknowledged the change in atmosphere, and began activating programs throughout its body. Oxar stared at the liquid in his cup after being threatened, knowing that danger was imminent. Pandora, however, kept her eyes on Champ.

"Why?" Pandora asked as Champ put his empty cup on the ground.

"Why, what?" he asked in reply, looking up at her.

"Why are you going to kill us?" she enquired, "You know who we are, why we're here and why we're doing it. So, why are you standing in our way?" Champ looked at her briefly before staring into the flames, sitting back, and nodding slowly before his previous smile returned and he turned to face her.

"Because I enjoy it," he stated, before jumping forward at her, pushing them both to the ground. Pandora hit the floor with a thud, knocking the wind out of her system as Champ continued his journey to land on her.

Trigger fired nir rifle, but Champ pushed his full weight into Pandora's shoulders with his hands, rolling forwards, and avoiding the shot. Once he'd hit the ground, Champ sprinted into the darkness, as R9 and Oxar rose to their feet.

"Where is he?" Trigger shouted, reloading quickly whilst Oxar pulled Pandora to her feet. R9's eyes glowed brightly as it stared into the shadows.

"He's on the wall there," R9 declared, pointing to his position above them. Trigger aimed where R9 had directed then pulled the trigger, the soft, fleshy *smack* informed the group that the bullet had hit its mark. Pandora breathed a sigh of relief.

"He's coming," R9 stated, moments before Champ swooped at the group, blood trickling down one of his wings, and grabbed hold of R9's head, before they both disappeared into the shadows.

"Holy Zxaperia!" Trigger shouted, dropping nir rifle and pulling out nir pistols, "I can't see him!" The wheels span in Pandora's mind as she picked up one of the bentwood chairs.

"Oxar, set this alight!" she commanded, holding it away from her. Oxar nodded, and his mouth inflated with gas before something in his throat clicked and he roared flames at the innocent wooden chair, setting the back ablaze. Champ yelled in the darkness, providing Pandora a target as she hurled the chair in that direction. The new flames lit up another area of the room, allowing the trio to see Champ and R9; R9 had wrapped its limbs around Champ's arm, and whilst Champ was blinded by the sudden light, a bone-snapping crack bounced off of the stone walls as Champ's grip broke on R9's head and it fell to the ground. Bellowing, Champ leapt at the wall and climbed up the flat surface, returning to the shadows, his broken arm hanging by his side.

Oxar and Pandora nodded at one another before setting ablaze the remaining five chairs and throwing them across the room, whilst R9 returned to the safety of the group.

"I love it when they put up a challenge," Champ said, menacingly, accompanied by a soft pitter-patter as the blood from his wounds dripped to the ground.

"Then you're going to love us!" Trigger replied, firing four rounds in the direction of his voice. Champ chuckled as the bullets smashed harmlessly into the solid rock. Trigger gritted nir teeth, whispering, "Where'd he go?" R9 looked up at the walls, trying to find him but coming away with nothing.

Suddenly, Champ landed in front of Trigger, his skin had changed to a stone-like tone.

"What the…!" Trigger began but was cut short by Champ, as he smashed the back of his hand into nir cheek, sending nem flying. Oxar stepped up next, grabbing Champ by the neck and breathing in, preparing to breathe fire, but Champ reacted faster, spitting an inferno into Oxar's face, setting his furred head ablaze. Oxar yelled; releasing his grip as his smothered the flames with his hands, whilst Champ cracked Oxar in the ribs with his knee. Turning to face R9 again, Champ scowled, grabbing hold of its throat.

"I've always hated robots," Champ announced, beginning to crush the metallic throat in his hand.

"Why?" R9 replied calmly, "We provide such useful distractions." Champ's face fell as he felt both of Pandora's stone blades sink into his upper trapezium muscles. His grip weakened as the blades were forced down, severing his nerves and splitting his veins. Champ fell to his knees, a smile on his face as he began to chuckle through the pain.

"You, you really were a challenge," Champ stated between breaths of laughter.

"Affirmative," R9 replied, curling its hand into a pointed fist and driving it into Champ's face, smashing through his skull and destroying the brain in a single punch. Champ fell sideways, unrecognisable. Silence fell as the fires flickered; each slowly turning blue as their heat increased, as the group re-joined around Champ's body it began to crackle, setting itself alight with the same blue flames.

After a few moments of steady breathing, Trigger was the first to move to the grand spiral staircase and begin the long ascent, the others followed swiftly. The staircase led up to a trapdoor that opened to the rooftop. As they emerged, the white flag stood proudly in front of them, waving happily at this heightened altitude, whilst to their left and right were two chests baring the respective symbols of either the Solar or Nocturnal teams. Trigger scrambled to the Solar's chest, attempting to heave it open, but ne was being stopped by the locked mechanism that kept its content sealed tightly inside. Oxar did the same to the Nocturnal marked chest, but also received the same result. Pandora walked forward, whilst R9 held the door open, and grabbed hold of the flag with her bloody hand. As she did, the flag changed as expected, and the Solar's chest clicked open.

Trigger ripped the chest open and browsed at the content. Ne reached inside and with a smile pulled out nir pair of black revolvers, with white handles. Ne tossed away the ones ne had found in Run-Down Town, and slipped nir custom revolvers into the holsters, feeling a lot more like nir old self. Returning to the chest, ne then pulled out a small black messenger bag, which was deceptively heavy.

"My bag!" Pandora smiled, running over and taking it from Trigger, quickly opening it to see that all her belongings were still inside. Trigger smiled at her reaction, before plunging in again, and returning with a blooded pair of knuckledusters, and turning to Oxar with a raised eyebrow.

"There's a difference between fighting and what we

have to do here," Oxar stated taking the knuckledusters from nem, as nir eyes darted around his bare face and torso and noticing the small scars that laced his body, that had been hidden beneath the short layer of fur.

Pandora looked into the chest and spotted the Rip Jaw dagger that must have belonged to their missing fourth official member. Reaching in, she picked it up and examined the lightweight blade, with one finger; she traced up the blade but pulled away quickly as the edge sliced open her finger.

"Broadcasted information from Kaio, stated that two players were pulled out of the game," R9 stated, watching Pandora's curiosity, "One from each team." She nodded, slipping the blade into the adjustable scabbard she had fixed to the outside of her bag.

R9's head clicked up to the sky as it connected to Professors wireless information distribution network which was informing the other R-units of her plan and location.

"Team Nocturnal are waiting outside," R9 declared.

Team Solar nodded at one another, wiping away any visible blood.

Oxar slipped his fingers into his prized knuckledusters.

R9 moved aside to let them pass then they all descended, to meet their opponents.

Chapter Thirteen
When the Moon Met the Sun

Gronix stood staring at the large wooden doors of Central Tower, speculating if the creature that had destroyed R4 had turned his opponents into a red sludge, or if they had killed the 'Champ' creature that dwelled within. Omiss emerged through the closed door, blood dripping from his mouth and hands.

"The deceased creature was not the one of those from the broadcast," Omiss stated, before licking his fingers, having enjoyed another delicious substance Vanicrast had to offer. Between licks, he looked up at his summoner and realised that he wanted more information, after sucking the blood off his left thumb he continued, "The pack had reached the top of the tower when I arrived, so they may be some time."

"Thank you," Gronix said, re-reading the words scribed upon the wooden panels. This 'Champ' creature, son of Kaio, was believed to be powerful enough to hold a landmark of this island, deemed capable to hold its own against the murderous players of the game, yet it had been defeated by Team Solar, without them having any casualties of their own. Omiss yawned wiping his lips with the back of its hands as his meal began to ooze out of the bottom of his midsection, his bowel movement complete.

"Tell me again, why are we out here ready to die, whilst that science bitch is still back in her lab?" Murados asked, before pressing her tongue against her furred forearm and licking up to her wrist. She then proceeded to use her moist forearm to wipe her thick, black hair out of her face.

Omiss sank back into the door as Gronix glanced at the feline-humanoid before replying, "Put simply, because we can kill things and she is more useful creating things that help us to do that."

Murados sighed, wiping the remnant saliva from her arm. The Golden Grimalkin that she had killed on their journey had not agreed with her acquired taste palette, and now her instinctual desire to be clean was beginning to bother her. She could feel Gronix's gaze upon her, felt his eyes drifting up her furred body, from her pawed feet, past the thin golden pelt that outlined her muscular stomach and the black mane-like hair that snaked its way over her shoulders and bosom, and finally landing on her face. She flicked her eyes in his direction, catching his head quickly turn away to stare at the wooden door once more.

"Why are we stood so close to the door?" Murados questioned, looking down the two stone walls of the tower that they could see from the grand, corner entrance.

"And where would you suggest would be the best place for us to strike?" Gronix replied, his fingers twitching, ready for the duel at hand.

"Literally anywhere," Murados responded, examining her fingers as her claws extended and retracted, "Where's the element of surprise?"

"They know we're here," Gronix murmured, as Omiss returned silently, floating round the pair before stopping between them. Before Gronix could question Team Solar's progress, he heard the echo of a something heavy smash against the floor inside the building.

Gronix closed his eyes momentarily, whispering a simple combat spell that had saved his life countless times previously. The door let out a rebellious creak as it was pushed open from within, Gronix readied himself for the imminent battle. His tongue darted around his mouth as he began another spell, his shoulder coming in as he curled his fingers and brought his hand slightly closer to his chest. His blackened fingertips glowed white as the spell activated, then in one smooth action, Gronix threw his hand forward hurling a blast of ice at his opponent, and hitting... nothing.

R9 was crouched on all fours, one of its hands next to the now open door. In the momentary stillness, Gronix stared at the robotic being in confusion and anger, but this was short-lived as the Minotaur landed on Omiss, crushing the demon into the earth. Gronix and Murados stumbled backwards as the huge mass began to stand, Omiss sinking into the earth beneath him. Murados moved first, darting forward in the blink of an eye and striking at Oxar's face, her claws tearing into his cheek. Gronix gritted his teeth as he brought his palms together and began a new incantation, before spinning off balance as a bullet smashed into the protective barrier he'd created.

Regaining his footing, he heard the click of a firearm being reloaded. Snapping round, hand ablaze, Gronix yelled a fire spell at the source of the shot. The fireball sped towards Trigger, lighting up the shadows as it flew across the tower interior. Trigger quickly rolled out of the way, diving off of nir elevated position on the staircase. Inhaling, Gronix looked over at Murados darting around Oxar's powerful swings; a fight of agility verses strength.

Suddenly, he felt the cold metallic grip of R9's robotic fingers around his throat, the android popping up from its crawling position. Scowling, Gronix drove his flamed hand into R9's face, wrapping his fingers around its positronic brain and melting it in his grasp. R9's green eyes faded to black as its processors failed to keep its programmes active. Tearing his fist out of the robot's skull, R9's legs buckled beneath it, falling away from the warlock.

"No!" a feminine voice screamed from the doorway. Gronix looked up at the voice, and spotted the slim half-elf, tightly clutching a Rip Jaw dagger, her eyes locked onto him. She charged at Gronix, but he smiled in reply, raising his hand and whispering his most recent, favourite spell. A purple, empty spiral appeared out of thin air directly behind her spine, her eyes snapped open as the spiral grew long tendrils that latched onto her clothing, stopping her in her tracks and pulling her back into its nothingness; some part of her realised the inevitability of what would happen next.

By the time Pandora had inhaled, the spiral had hooked onto her skin, its dark fingers digging into her muscles as it dragged her off of her feet. As she exhaled, its dark tentacles had wormed their way around her stomach. Pandora clenched her jaw to keep herself from screaming as the spiral opened slightly wider, like a snake preparing for a large meal. Gronix watched with dead eyes and a smile of glee, he had watched this show a few times before, yet it always amused him at how long the victim would attempt to appear strong in the face of certain death.

A bullet whizzed past Pandora's head and through Gronix's open palm, spraying his face with blood. Gronix roared; nursing his hand against his chest as he looked behind Pandora at the approaching gunner, who was slipping nir rifle into its holster as ne sprinted toward the battlefield. Glancing again at Murados and the bloodied Oxar, Gronix began to retreat from the violence.

As he watched, Oxar outreached his left hand into the empty air and caught Murados arm as she tried to whip around him. Slamming his right hand into her side, Oxar lifted Murados off her feet, her speed useless in midair. Murados struggled against his grip, but to no avail. Oxar leant back slightly before he smashed his thick head into Murados's. After first contact, Oxar turned his head quickly, his horns slicing through Murados's flesh like butter. Gronix swallowed, realising he was now alone in his effort, as Oxar lifted Murados high in the air, before smashing the feline-humanoid doll into the earth.

Gronix's eyes darted back to the advancing gunner, as Trigger drew nir twin pistols. His voiceless lips rattled off with his least favourite spell, instinct informing him what would happen to him next. Nearing the end of his incantation, his eyes fell upon Pandora once more. The spiral had forced her spine to break in such a way that she was staring at him, between her feet. He smiled as he finished his spell and Trigger came round Pandora, revolvers already aimed at Gronix, nir fingers pulled back both the triggers, the two bullets smashed into Gronix's head and heart.

Gronix was thrown onto the ground dead by the force of the shots, whilst Pandora was sprayed with blood. Blood trickled down the back of Triggers head and back, frowning ne turned to Pandora, who tried to inhale again. An empty bullet wound had appeared in Triggers forehead, and another in her chest directly above nir heart. Trigger fell to nir knees, as Gronix's spell took its full affect, killing nem in the same way that he had died. Ne looked up at the folded Pandora, as the spiral began to engulf her body, and smiled weakly, attempting to comfort them both in this fatal moment. A tear ran down Pandora's cheek as she stroked the bloody top of Trigger's head. Finally, the spiral swallowed the half-elf, and nir wounds became too much for Trigger. Then only silence remained.

Oxar stood alone, frozen in shock; the sole survivor of the battle at Central Tower. His wounds bled steadily as he shook, the adrenaline subsiding as his senses returned, and he began his journey west, towards the valley.

As he walked, a black hand silently erupted out of the soil and pulled an angered demon back to the surface.

Chapter Fourteen
Famine Valley

Oxar wiped his brow of sweat and blood as he passed between two of the many mountains that stood like guards across the land. The flow of blood had ceased, with much of it drying on his skin, clumping and pulling at his fur as he moved, and producing an iron scent that clung to his nostrils in the dry environment. When he reached the other side of the mountains, he was faced with a sharp drop as the mountains laced either bank of the deep valley that cut across most of the island. Oxar sat for a moment, tearing some familiar looking plant life out of the soil and draining the sweet liquid from within its stem. Breathing slowly, his vision cleared slightly, helping him to see a white flag wave merrily in the distance. Oxar rolled his aching joints, gritting his teeth to the pain as his partially closed wounds threatened to reopen and continue their attempt to release all of his blood. Sucking in a lungful of air, Oxar stepped over the edge, and braced for landing.

He regretted his decision when he hit the uneven ground at the bottom of the valley. From the top of the valley, Oxar couldn't see the different elevations of earth, so when he hit the ground with his left foot much sooner than his right, his left leg compressed like a spring, and Oxar bounced away from his landing point, crashing against a camouflaged boulder a few feet away. He lay still for a few moments, the boulder resting against his left shoulder, as he stared up at the clear sky and tried to calm his aching mind, and screaming muscles.

As he lay there, he heard a familiar noise, from before this brutal game; the soft beat of an agile creature investigating Oxar's presence. He felt its hot breath warm his fingers as in sniffed at his scent, assessing if he was still alive, and if he was a threat. He felt its razor sharp teeth graze his exposed stomach, causing it to twitch involuntarily. Stillness. Then Oxar felt a sudden uncomfortable yet strangely comforting weight as the beast lay its head upon his chest.

Looking down, he stared into the eyes of a Golden Grimalkin; a breed similar to the Websting Grimalkins Oxar had travelled with during his time in Henthaa. Oxar had learnt a lot about Grimalkins whilst in Henthaa, where he had been welcomed in by an arachne family, who accepted his beastly appearance that paled in comparison to their arachnid-humanoid form. They had taught him that once a Grimalkin had created kinship with another individual, its scent would linger over its friend for many years, preventing it from being killed by another Grimalkin, who would instead recognise the individual as a friend to its livelihood.

Oxar reached out a cautious hand and stroked the beautiful creature's black mane; smearing blood into its dark fur, the creature closed its eyes and relaxed. Oxar could sense that it had lost another of its kind recently, and was seeking as much comfort as he was. The Golden

Grimalkin were pack animals, creating lifetime bonds with their companions, that were so strong that the species was believed to have gone extinct when a large portion of the breed had died in the Grothaig Hellfire.

Yawning, the Grimalkin stretched it spine, then rose, standing expectantly over him, waiting for Oxar to stand also. He pushed himself to his feet slowly, the adrenaline that had eased his pain on impact had diluted to nothingness, and Oxar was left in his weakened state that reflected a strong human. The Golden Grimalkin grunted at Oxar, nudging his open hand; bringing a smile to the Minotaur's pained expression.

It felt like an age had passed when Oxar finally reached the foot of the tall rock formation that held the flag proudly. When Oxar had gotten close enough, the proximity sensors detected him and activated Kaio's holographic message. He stood before Oxar, wearing a fake set of white wings, like the ones his mother had once worn to one of the castle balls.

"Welcome Warrior, to Famine Valley," Kaio smiled, "The flag for this location is on top of the formation behind me, the highest point inside the valley, but don't go too high, don't forget the rules." Oxar frowned at Kaio's closing warning, before watching him look up to the sky and then sink into the ground, causing Oxar to let out a weak chuckle. Oxar stared up at the stone tower, and sighed, questioning his ability to scale the vertical and concaved surfaces.

The Grimalkin grunted once more, turning its back on Oxar before it dashed off in search of another pack to join. Oxar watched the beast until it was merely a golden glint on the horizon, a sadness welling inside of him as he stood alone once more. He had spent so much of his life alone, hiding from others, fearful of how they would react; so far the track record for humanoid friendship had always been less than appealing.

Swallowing, Oxar looked up at the formation once more. Rolled his shoulders, and began the deadly climb. Once he had run out of natural foot-holes to take advantage of, Oxar began making his own, smashing his knuckledusters into the solid rock to create gaps in the stone. Yet, with each strike he could feel his muscles cry in pain, and he knew that he would not be able to continue clinging to the stone, with his blooded fingers, for much longer. When he glanced up, the stone wall seemed to stretch endlessly to the sky, further out of his grasp, yet glancing down he was met with a similar misjudgement of distances, the ground seeming to be hundreds of miles below him, even though he knew that the entire formation was no taller that a palace spire, Oxar began to fear falling from this height in his current state.

Reaching the peak, Oxar was faced with a beautiful view, unlike at the top of Central Tower; he was able to see more than just clouds. From here, the view was bordered with mountains but he could see thick woodland to the north, and looking west he could see a small black castle wall complete with a moat, and some sort of building with a giant telescope to the south the castle. Looking back to where he had come from, Oxar smiled at the small river that separated Central Tower from Run-Down Town, the volcano in the distance that Pandora had spoken of, and the stone maze that he'd been rescued from.

Turning on the spot, Oxar finally stopped in front of the white flag of Famine Valley. Against his own beliefs, he'd conquered the challenge that was set out in front of him, and although his body threatened to quit on him, Oxar forced his arm out and gripped the white flag in his fingers. The flag burst into colour, bringing another smile to his face.

Breathing deeply, Oxar let go of the flag and stepped backwards. He felt something grab hold of his ankle. Looking down, he saw a black hand gripping his leg tightly. He didn't have time to react. The hand pulled Oxar back, and the Minotaur fell from the formation, powerless against the wind that caused him to tumble, he landed with a deafening snap.

His body screamed, and then, only a humoured, blood-thirsty silence remained.

Chapter Fifteen
Solar Advertisement Break

Kaio stood in the centre of the Green Room, the camera pod circling up him slowly as dramatic music played, intending to cause excitement for the viewers. When the pod reached his face, the automated audience cheered loudly for a moment, before Kaio clicked his fingers, muting the audience, and smiled at the camera.

"Good morning, people of Vanicrast," Kaio said, "I hope that you've been enjoying this season of *Eclipse*. I've recorded our highest ratio of desired viewership, compared to those who have tried to switch off, unplug or cover their televisions, since I began this show. Which I just think is amazing." A large genuine smile slipped onto Kaio's face, his attempt at helping was finally being accepted by the majority of viewers.

"Now, I know I ended yesterday's broadcast on a bit of a cliff-hanger, and I heard many of you yelling in frustration of being forced to wait for the continuation of those events." Kaio spoke confidently, pushing his hair out of his face, "But after the loving response of the last commercial break, I've decided to create some more. So, without wasting more of your time; here's what I've come up with…" Kaio clapped his hands, and the green room engulfed him, before it turned black.

***

The room transformed into a dimly-lit, basement office, in Yanstag. Kaio was sat behind the office desk, relaxing in a leather armchair with his smart black shoes, with red laces, resting upon the table.

"Have you ever needed something that you couldn't get yourself?" Kaio asked, as the camera pod approached slowly, "Wanted something someone else had? Wished that your neighbour's revival crystal was your revival crystal?" He took his feet off the table, and leant over the thin folders that littered the desk.

"Well, if you have the coin, we can provide the service. Here at Sell-Thieves, we can guarantee the theft of any property that you request, for the right amount of money. Our previous successful robberies include; the central jewel from King Xavier's crown, the golden war dagger of Higlo and the rights to King Raddis's private holiday island.

"Sell-Thieves in Yanstag, between 'Stab-a-lot's' and 'Candy Treats', open whenever the boss says so. We look forward to stealing for you." Kaio winked, leaning back again as the camera pod retreated from the room, the door closing behind it.

***

When the door re-opened, the room was flooded and Kaio stood submerged, a clear respirator covering his mouth and nose.

"Are you looking for cheap real estate?" Kaio asked

sincerely, "With the housing market in the state it is right now, buyers are snatching all the land they can get their hands on, are you planning to be left behind? If you answered no, you're in luck! Ingswa is still ripe with property up for grabs."

The background shifted from endless ocean, to an image of the underwater land of Ingswa.

"Ingswa, home of the trustworthy aquaticans, these properties are built to withstand rain, sleet, hurricanes, lightning and being submerged 347 days of the year. These properties are the perfect holiday homes for those who are unable to breathe underwater, complete with their own armed forces to keep you safe whilst you're sightseeing this magical land." Kaio smiled, "You could visit King Raddis and Queen Viron, ride on the backs of Rip Jaws, take part in practise duels with their specially trained forces, take in the rich aquatic culture, and also view one of the countless battles between Ingswa and the barbaric forces of Grothaig."

"Ingswa," Kaio concluded, "Why don't you already have a home here?" The room began to cloud, as the water evaporated into steam at an accelerated rate.

***

The camera pod panned over the western terrain of Riodic, swooping over the desert with dotted patches where little towns had been settled.

"First discovered by elves, Riodic was first seen as a land of opportunity; the massive amounts of untapped potential, land, crops, water and no human overlords controlling everything." Kaio's disembodied voice announced, "But coming this never, a story about a little boy... a little girl... a little individual whose journey for food caused them to travel to Vilderton, and fall through time!"

The camera began following a covered youth, as ne travelled across the sands and to the city of Vilderton, finding shelter from a sandstorm within one of the small abandoned buildings on the outskirts of the town, and falling asleep.

The lights flashed brightly, waking the sleeper, who immediately rose and pulled the door open to see Dystopia.

"A journey of discovery, friendship, and guns!" Kaio continued, as snippets of the youth's adventures flashed on the screen, showing fragmented scenes of the fictional documentary film. "Introducing, Trigger as Trigger, and Kaio as everyone else. A Kaio production, *The Grand, The Evil, and The Timeless*. Coming nowhere, never."

The screen faded to black, showing only the title screen, with Trigger's face visible behind the letters. The automated audience cheered as the fake trailer ended.

***

Machinery switched on in the darkness, the soft metallic scraping sounded as metal cogs grinded against each other, a melodic puff of smoke bursting from a nearby vent. A single hanging bulb flicked into existence, lighting up a wooden box in the dark environment. The noises stopped, and a gentle red glow began emanating from inside the crate. There was a quiet click, before the wooden crate burst open; the shiny beast within escaping its flimsy prison. The bulb swung weakly in the air, knocked by a stray fragment of wood, its light reflecting off the humanoids' metallic skin.

"The R-Unit is our latest line in Professor Products," Kaio's disembodied voice announced, "Complete with the latest developments in Vanicrast technology, the R-Units, are capable of accomplishing any task given to them." The R-Unit stared outwards, past the camera, as the swaying light lit up its branded shoulder and chest plate, revealing the solid black R0 marking.

"Also, for our more *sunny* customers, the R-Unit's are also available," Kaio continued, the R-Unit's eyes turned green and looked into the camera lens, "Freed and Independent. The closest a being can be to human without a beating heart."

"The R-Unit, only five Kaio Coins, at your local Professor Products seller," Kaio finished. The R-Unit raised its left hand, its eyes turning red as it caught the swinging bulb. Then, still staring into the camera, the R-Unit crushed the light source in its hand, returning the environment to the still silent darkness previously established.

***

A spotlight clicked on over a screaming toddler in a cradle, attached to the cradle was a sign saying; Prince of Borantik. The prince was hooked up to a blood bag, and was obviously ill in appearance. Before the silent crowd, two humanoids snuck onto the stage with a second blood bag, this one labelled with a stencil of a generic Minotaur head. The crowd gasped in shock as the pair switched the blood bags, and the toddler's screams ceased.

"Records are sketchy about the disappearance of the Borantik Prince," Kaio stated, as the cradle fell towards the audience, and the toddler stepped out. As they watched, the boy's blonde hair darkened to a shade of russet, and the seeds of two horns began pushing against the skin of his forehead.

"It is known that the prince was not born the monster he ran away as," Kaio continued, "King Xavier and Queen Eleck, loved their son, but after the operation to save his life had been sabotaged, they knew the public would not fully accept his new image. So, instead they chose to keep the boy locked within the eastern wing of their palace, until they found a medical, or magical, way of helping their child return to his previous form." As Kaio spoke, the boy grew a few years, his horns growing to a respectable length for his age, and his appearance darkening as fur covered his skin.

"However, during the masked celebration of Estafer, the door to his wing was left unlocked, and a young Minotaur Prince left the established safety to investigate the ball that had taken a hold over the kingdom. Yet, when he emerged from his wing..." Kaio's voice was overshadowed by screams, as masked dancers appeared onstage and noticed the toddler and became fearful of his presence. This in turn terrified the boy who tried to run back to his door, but other dancers had already circled round to the door, seeking the safety of having the solid wall against their back. Crying the boy, looked around the sea of faces attempting to spot his parents, but he could not hear their calls over the dancers' screams and yells. Eventually, one of the male dancers went to assault the weeping boy, but feeling threatened the prince ran out of the ball, and fled the courtyard, sprinting into the darkness.

"Records of the prince's travels are sketchy, he is believed to have been sighted near Elkanner and Grothaig, although upon investigation, the search parties have still been unable to detect the lost Prince of Borantik," Kaio spoke sadly, "If you believe you have any information, please contact any guardsmen of Borantik, a reward for the prince's return is available. Even after these many years, the King and Queen are still waiting in hope for their son to come back to them."

***

The Green Room re-materialised once more with Kaio stood in the centre of the room, smiling proudly before speaking,

"Well, that was fun. I hope you enjoyed it.
And now, to the real event:
Eclipse! Season seventeen!
Broadcasting;
Right Now!"

Chapter Sixteen
Night Terrors

Omiss lay under the soil below the Minotaur, his body damaged by the impact force of having such a heavy weight smash onto his ill prepared form. He questioned how he had managed to be tricked by such an obvious manoeuvre, one that he himself had used countless times before in the Nightmare Plains. He missed the Nightmare Plains.

Vanicrast held many delights for him, the smells and tastes that danced across his palette, the blood he'd consumed and the creatures he'd killed whilst serving his mortal summoner, but these beings were ready for battle. Most of the creatures on Blue Crystal Island had concluded that they were in a kill or be killed environment; meaning Omiss couldn't play with his food like he had done during previous summonings.

Omiss swished blood around in his mouth, not his own, but the remnants of his earlier meal that had been pushed up into his throat by the Minotaur's actions. Swallowing, he felt his skin knit back together, the red liquid reacting with his internal systems, and creating an immense amount of energy that was quickly dispersed and fed to the damaged areas of his tattered being. His thoughts reeled through the many times he'd allowed his victims to punish him in Zxaperia before he'd pull the rug from beneath their feet and remind them how powerful he truly was, but on Vanicrast, he could feel himself weakening with each hour that he did not consume.

There was silence above him. No longer could he hear the stomps and yells of battle on the surface. Omiss licked his lips as he pushed his blackened hand up to the surface, pulling himself back to the world above. Looking at the battlefield, anger bubbled inside of him for missing such a bloodbath. His summoner laid on his back a few feet away, a bullet hole in his forehead and his cloak drenched in blood. Omiss sighed, knowing that he would be blamed for this death. His eyes swept across the scene, spotting the corpses of the R-9 unit and one of the other Solar Team members beside a large puddle of thick blood laced with purple mucus. Finally his gaze landed on his old pet: Miranda 'Murados' Sty.

Omiss had been unable to not smile at the woman, each and every time he'd seen her, remembering their time together in Zxaperia. Images flickered through his mind as he recalled their time together; the time he'd torn her skin off piece by piece, the time he'd presented her with her family then made them melt in front of her eyes, and, his personal favourite; the time he made her kill others for his amusement under the guise that she would be spared. Of course, those memories were left in Zxaperia for her, but Omiss would chuckle to himself when he watched them briefly show themselves in her sub-conscious, causing her to shiver at the sight of him.

Omiss noticed that something was missing, a conflict involving six others but there were only four bodies and a puddle left by the fifth. Omiss frowned, his eyes analysing the battlefield as his mind created images of the fight; Gronix shutdown the robot, then hurled a spell at the girl, but was killed by the gunslinger, who then killed nemself? Whilst the Minotaur fought with Murados, won the fight and... Omiss's eyes landed on the sprinkling of blood that wandered around the corpses before scarpering from the Tower towards Famine Valley.

After devouring a portion of warlock's brain, Omiss's meal was stolen from him by time. The corpses of battle dissolved into powder before his eyes, one by one beginning with the robot. Angered by the turn of events, Omiss turned to the true task at hand and followed the blood trail towards the mountains.

The Minotaur was easy to track; its wounds had refused to close during much of the journey, and its large prints disturbed the earth vividly. Omiss suspected that his target was dead when he finally caught up with him, the Minotaur laid on the ground covered in blood, with a Golden Grimalkin burrowing its face into the beast's stomach, appearing to be feasting on his insides. However, as Omiss approached the Grimalkin rose and glared at him, its yellow eyes piercing Omiss's as it patiently guarded the Minotaur as he clambered to his feet. Omiss halted in his journey, choosing to observe rather than go in for the kill, believing it to be more use to gather information, although it would be more fun to kill the Minotaur and be done with it.

The Minotaur seemed to be fond and respectful of the beast, the Grimalkin reflecting his own animalistic nature, Omiss assumed, yet, strangely, the Grimalkin seemed to reciprocate. It never left the Minotaur's side as Omiss stalked the pair, occasionally it would bear its teeth at him; until they reached the foot of a grand stone tower, and the beast could follow no further. The Minotaur activated Kaio's message, explaining the usual game related drivel, before he sunk into the earth. The Minotaur and Grimalkin exchanged a look, and then the beast turned to face Omiss and charged towards him.

Omiss sighed at this futile attempt, but entertained the creature's primal mind by creating an empty copy of himself which fled from it, whilst the original submerged and advanced towards the weakened Minotaur.

***

The formation summit would have been beautiful to another, but to Omiss it merely showed the limitations of his chains, unable to truly explore whilst bound to a summoner. As he looked into the sun, Omiss contemplated if he had ever really experienced freedom since his creation. Lord Termin had sculpted his form, breathed life into his body, moulded his mind as a pale reflection of his Lord's, and had then thrown him into work at the Nightmare Plains, playing with the tortured souls of those that had lived before, for the amusement of his Lord. Then, whenever he was called, Omiss was forced to act on behalf of a mortal, chained to their side until release or permanent death of either party.

Omiss recollected the first time he had been summoned to Vanicrast. A young warlock girl, with a speech impediment, had discovered one of her father's scrolls, and against all odds, she had managed to pronounce each word of the chant correctly, before placing a piece of string in her mouth. Melody Able had wanted a friend whilst she and her family travelled in Henthaa, and had believed that the summoning scroll labelled "Nightmare Plain Demon", was the reasonable choice. It didn't work out, her speech made her childish requests inaudible to Omiss, who was more interested in the new world around him than what some child was trying to get him to do. He'd gotten a taste of Vanicrast's wonders, even getting as far as tasting his first malus, he still remembered the succulent juices of the fruit running down his chin as he bit through its crunchy skin, but then he was tossed back into Zxaperia, by the girl's father reversing the charm.

The Minotaur's bloodied hand reached over the edge, signalling to Omiss that it was time to play. Disappearing into the rock, he observed the Minotaur as he looked out across the horizon before capturing the white flag for his team, and then, when the Minotaur had stepped back towards the ledge, Omiss struck. Omiss grabbed hold of the Minotaur's leg and pulled himself into the creature.

The force of his actions forced them into a downwards spiral towards the ground below, powerless to combat gravity, before the Minotaur's body smashed into the solid earth with a deafening snap. Omiss smiled from within Oxar's mind, watching its soul curl up in pain and scream silently. Omiss shook his head; this had only wounded the beast, and although the wounds would kill it, Omiss would play with his prey a little more before death finally took hold.

Clicking his fingers, Omiss made Oxar believe they were still on the summit; his soul wiped its stained cheeks, while its body's screams continued unheard to the preoccupied mind. Before them were the same beautiful views they had witnessed moments before, but suddenly something familiar glinted on one of the valley edges below Oxar. Turning to face it, he spotted the metallic reflection of Trigger's rifle on one of the mountains that lined the valley, aimed at him. Oxar frowned, confused by Triggers actions, with no reason to think them false. The Trigger illusion fired nir rifle, blowing Oxar off his feet and hurling him to the ground below once more. Licking his lips, Omiss snapped his fingers again, and Oxar's mind was beaten with two helpings of the fall, and the heartbreak of being shot by his ally.

Omiss laughed as he repeated the illusion, letting each of Oxar's team members murder him before his inevitable fall, beating him with the gradually escalating pain.

Before long, the true fall damage took its toll, Oxar's blood flow slowed as less was contained within his body. Finally, the Minotaur closed his eyes from the pain. A fictional, murderous Grimalkin disappeared from existence.

Death took hold, and Omiss enjoyed a free ride back to Solar HQ.

Chapter Seventeen
Betrayal in the Darkness

Gronix sat on his bed, the pale moonlight illuminating the textbook in his hands, as his eyes hungrily gobbled up the information on the pages. The textbook contained spells that his class wouldn't even be considering for another year, yet here he was, learning it as easily as if were a simple levitation charm. Looking up from the book, Gronix selected a target for his experiment. His eyes landed on the malformed arachne warrior action-figure that stood guard at the foot of his bed, a treasure he'd discovered in the college's lost and found box in his first week, which had since been the guinea pig for many charms, curses and incantations.

Straightening up, but keeping the book in the light, Gronix prepared himself. Extending his palm towards his toy, he breathed in deeply before speaking clearly.

"Fiss-Ca," Gronix whispered, questioning the pronunciation of the words as they left his lips. The action-figure rattled softly against the solid wood, before it expanded, its small plastic features ballooning, within moments the previously eight inch figurine stood at a height of two foot. Gronix smiled at his success, but then he realised that the expansion process was not slowing.

Licking his lips nervously, his eyes darted to the page in his hand. He scanned the page quickly, but came back empty handed. However, he noticed that the previous reader had dog-eared the page, pairing it with another a few sheets deeper. Flicking his wrist, Gronix arrived at a page filled with small printed text, with a single word in bold, highlighting it against the rest. Without consideration, Gronix spoke the word.

"Bola-Gar," he mumbled, his shaking hand still extended to the expanding target. The arachne stopped growing, looming over Gronix in the shadows. Gronix breathed a sigh of relief before he noticed the soft whistling coming from the giant doll. Frowning, Gronix approached the action-figure and discovered a small slit in the figure's torso. Raising an eyebrow, he covered the slit with his finger, holding in the air that was pushing its way out of the slowly deflating doll, and the whistling stop. Gronix smiled, and then the arachne warrior exploded.

Gronix held his scream in his throat, but he knew it was too late, he could already hear the rumblings downstairs as his drunken father awakened from the sudden noise. Gronix leapt beneath his bed covers and prayed, holding the textbook to his chest.

"What was that?" Tarroscan called from his bedroom door, Gronix's elder brother had also been woken by the explosion. Gronix shut his eyes tightly as he heard the stomping of his father unsteadily ascend the staircase. The silence lasted an age, as Gronix waited for the inevitable, he yawned as the passage of time seemed to linger.

"Gronix!" His father bellowed, throwing open the door, "What have I told you about practising spells at night?" He crossed the room in two strides and picked up the young warlock by the scruff of the neck with ease. His breath stank of Whystar mixed with Pride-catcher; the alcoholic stench shot up Gronix's nose and held his throat tightly.

"I've told you once, I've told you a thousand times!" his father roared. Tarroscan stood in the doorway, a smile plastered on his face. Gronix opened his mouth to respond but his father had already begun his next motion. Throwing Gronix away, he watched the boy fly into the wall behind him, the force knocking the wind out of the youth, the textbook bouncing onto the bed.

"You will do as you're told, boy!" his father yelled, grabbing Gronix by the scalp, "Or, I swear on your mother's grave, I will kill you. Understood?" Gronix held the hand tightly, every one of his father's swayed movements pulled at his hairs, causing his eyes to well up. His father did not enjoy the silent response, and yanked the boy's head back, forcing the child to look at him.

"I asked you a question, you good for nothing parasite!" he shouted, "Is that understood!?"

"Y-y-yes," Gronix replied, his eyes in danger of leaking at any moment.

"Yes, what?" His father asked, through gritted teeth.

"Yes, Father, I understand," Gronix replied, a tear rolling down his cheek. His father released his head, and skulked back to the door, his brother still smirking at the events. Gronix rubbed his aching scalp, wiping his tears with his sheets as he buried his face in his blankets. He heard the door slam shut as his family left him alone once more.

Just another night at the Void household.

***

"Top marks again, Gronix?" the Yanstag Mana Academy librarian asked, "And here I was thinking you were only pretending to read."

"I only pretend sometimes, Anasta," Gronix replied, smiling. The two shared a chuckle. Gronix loved the academy library; it was one of the biggest in Yanstag, with many first editions of rare manuscripts filling the grand bookshelves. He had always felt more at home with this paper palace of knowledge than with his father and brother, whose violent tendencies made Gronix question if he hadn't been swapped at birth, and that somewhere his real parents had been encumbered with a cruel brat.

"So, I suppose you want to flick through the new volumes that arrived today?" Anasta questioned, knowing that that was the only reason Gronix would be in the library before class.

"Well, if you're offering," Gronix smiled innocently, Anasta chuckled again, before placing her blackened palm under the desk and pushing the door release button.

"Go on then," Anasta said, "They're on the middle shelf, second case. Don't be too long, you don't want to be late for class."

"You know me, Anasta," Gronix said, opening the door, "Even if I were late, I already know it all." With that, Gronix slipped into the dimly lit storage room, where Anasta kept the new books, the damaged books, and the ones that were still being processed by the academies committee that certified any magic related book that may contain Dark Magic.

Following Anasta's instructions, Gronix found the

usual assortment of packages that held the written knowledge of those Gronix was inspired by. As he began rifling through the collection of latest tomes, his gaze locked onto the plain midnight blue cover of a book near the back of the bookcase. Picking it up, the thick volume felt light in his grasp, its blue cover mesmerising him as the light caused it to shimmer. Gronix held its spine loosely and let the leaves fall open onto a random page. As he read the words, Gronix felt them being etched into his long-term memory, and he quickly realised that this was one of the books that would be restricted to students. Yet, as he tried to pull away, his grip tightened, his eyes absorbed the information quicker, powerless against the book's desire to be read.

***

Gronix slowed his pace when he realised he would be home late. His father would already be home, Terroscan would be by his side, and they would both be intoxicated by this hour. As he arrived in front of his house, his suspicion was confirmed, as he heard Terroscan shout that, 'Gronix is late again'. Gronix swallowed, before pushing the door open.

"What time do you call this?" His father asked from his armchair, bottle in hand.

"I was finishing homework in the library," Gronix replied, avoiding eye contact with the drunken beast.

"We've heard that one before, eh, Dad?" Terroscan asked, trying to pour oil on the fire growing in their father's eyes.

"I didn't ask where you were, boy, I asked what time you call this. Now, answer the question," He demanded, his blurred gaze locked onto the slim warlock.

"I know I'm late," Gronix said quickly, hoping to avoid a confrontation, "I'm sorry." No sooner had the two words left his lips, was his father upon him, his thick fingers wrapped around Gronix's thin throat applying pressure as they pinned him to the door.

"You may be the most disappointing piece of filth in Yanstag," he whispered, "But you are still my son, and in this family; we never, *never*, say that word." Gronix clung onto his father's arm tightly, holding himself up as gravity threatened to strangle him. He released Gronix, letting him fall to the ground.

"To think, your mother died for you to live, and this is how you repay her?" He asked, throwing himself into his chair, "Pathetic."

"Fuck you," Gronix muttered, something snapping inside of him.

"What did you say to me?" His father scowled, preparing to get up again and remind Gronix who was in charge.

"I said, fuck you, old man," Gronix said, his voice laced with venom as his anger finally surfaced.

"Old man? Who the Zxaperia do you think you're talking to?" His father roared, rising to his feet. However, Gronix merely raised his left hand and his father was silenced, a sudden fearful expression on his face. Gronix felt the runes and words from the forbidden text emerge from his subconscious, and as he opened his right hand slowly; his father obediently opened his mouth, his eyes widening as he realised that his son had control over his body. Gronix slowly brought his right hand fingers together, as his father began to choke.

"Dad?" Terroscan asked, in an extremely worried

tone, slowly getting up. His father could only make strange guttural sounds in reply, before Gronix completed his curse. In one slow movement, Gronix shifted his palm from pointing at his suffocating father to the smoke-stained ceiling. Synchronised with Gronix's action, his father's mouth spewed out his organs, until his insides were outside of his body.

"Dad!" Terroscan screamed, as Gronix released his control, and his father fell to the floor in a weeping heap. After an age, the blood loss sank in, and slowly his father's whimpers turned to silence as he accepted the welcoming embrace of death. Terroscan wept silently before turning his gaze to Gronix.

"You!" Terroscan shouted, "You did this, didn't you? You horrible piece of sh…" Terroscan froze mid insult, as Gronix repeated the enchantment.

***

The blue revival crystal of Nocturnal Castle shone brightly, releasing a momentary beam of light that hit the courtyard floor, within the beam; physical coding streamed towards the lit circle creating the body and clothes of a recently deceased warlock.

"That could have gone better," Gronix sighed, getting off of the ground. A metallic figure stood near the door, its silver eyes locked onto Gronix.

"Professor's latest breed," Murados said, exiting the shadow to Gronix's left, her tail sweeping across the messy floor, "She got about halfway through the broadcast before it shut off. Said, she was going to use them to capture all the flags in one swoop."

"Clever," Gronix nodded, "So, we only have to

worry about the other team."

"It would seem that way," Murados said, edging closer, "Now, I need a favour."

"How do you mean?" Gronix asked, raising an eyebrow. Murados darted forward and latched her teeth into Gronix's throat.

"I need a more powerful form," Murados finished, pushing her black hair out of the way before chomping down on Gronix's throat, tearing open his windpipe.

Gronix fell to the ground, gasping for air.

Should have seen it coming, he thought.

The world began to dim, Murados began to transform, and Gronix experienced death once again.

Chapter Eighteen
Shattered Crystal

Sun Palace slowly illuminated as the Estafer shard began to glow, reviving the most recently deceased Solar team member. Slowly, Oxar was built within the soft blue beam that lit up a section of the damaged throne room. The repetitive toll of such a feat became obvious, as cracks began winding their way up the proud faces of the crystal.

Oxar gasped for air when the revival process had been completed, the light dimming around him until there was only a minor glow emanating from the crystal. He lay there for a moment, running his mind's eye over his body, focusing on the areas with previously broken bones, punctured skin and relentless bleeding. However, upon investigation he found that his body had been returned to the same healthy state as it had been before his involvement in *Eclipse*. Rising, Oxar noticed that his clothing was still damaged from his fights with Champ and the feline Nocturnal team member. Swallowing, Oxar thought back to the moments before his death; he had been at the Famine Valley flag and then… something had grabbed him? Or had someone shot him? Something had pounced onto him? The mixture of fractured memories confused the Minotaur, unable to put reality in focus.

In this moment, Omiss awoke from his slumber; the calm darkness of death had forced the demon into an unconscious state whilst within the Minotaur's mind. Looking at puzzled Oxar's soul, Omiss smiled, bearing his sharp teeth as he looked through the eyes of his unknowing host. Clicking his fingers, Omiss fabricated an enemy R-Unit standing on top of the crystal, staring down at newly reborn Minotaur.

Oxar heard the mechanical whirring of movement above him, as the R-Unit readied itself to jump down on the seemingly unaware beast. Breathing deeply, Oxar's face snapped skywards, his jaw dropped and a fiery blast burst from his mouth, narrowly missing the assailant, who had crouched down, clinging to the surface of the crystal as it scurried down to the ground. However, Oxar had anticipated this possible approach, and smashed his large, knuckleduster-wearing fist into the robot's spine. The robot's shell splintered on impact, the force breaking through its protective exoskeleton.

Chuckling, Omiss clicked his fingers once more, and the metallic creature faded into the nothingness it was created from. Oxar was left staring at his imbedded fist, his hand trapped to the wrist within the giant crystal, with its previously small cracks opening into deep ravines. Frowning, Oxar stared at the scene he was within, and began questioning reality once more; where had the robot gone? How had it disappeared? And what was that laughter he heard?

Then the penny dropped.

When he was a toddler, his mother had told him stories of demons; demons that were created in Zxaperia, creatures of darkness capable of causing visions and mirages, twisting the truth into a cruel fiction for their amusement. Oxar tore his hand out of the solid shard, the ravines deepening due to the sudden lack of support, and closed his eyes, pushing his fists together as he tried to focus. Omiss stopped laughing, as the optic windows shut but darkness did not embrace. Turning, Omiss watched as Oxar's soul turned to face the intruding monster.

In the Nightmare Plains, Omiss would have been able to conjure such impressive beasts as to halt the hosts attempt to reject his presence, but in the mortal world, Oxar had the advantage. His soul began to grow, its muscular form expanding until it towered over the 'powerful' demon. Its movements were slow and powerful, yet Omiss was unable to prevent them. In, one smooth motion, Oxar pounded Omiss to the ground, then picked him up and hurled him through the gaping hole of Oxar's open mouth.

As Omiss flew through the warm air within Sun Palace, Oxar's eyes snapped open and he grabbed hold of the hurtling demon, using its momentum to smash the monster, head first, into the cracked crystal. Dazed by the sudden turn of events, Omiss was unable to prevent Oxar's attacks, and the Minotaur took full advantage of that fact. Grasping the spirit by his neck and shoulder, Oxar mustered up all of his revived strength and pulled the two points away from each other, splitting Omiss in two.

Omiss screamed, experiencing pain he had never felt in the mortal world, and before the partition passed his chest, the demon fell silent. Oxar did not stop there though, tearing the monster into two separate halves.

Breathing deeply, Oxar hurled each piece of Omiss to either side of the room, its left side bounced into the corner near the door, whilst its right side smacked against the wounded crystal.

The crystal whined loudly at the impact, and creaked as Oxar stepped away from it, the ravines connecting with one another. As Oxar turned back to the moaning crystal, a light breeze passed through the open ceiling, and pushed against the giant shard, that was enough. Something collapsed within the crystal, and then the large Estafer shard shattered before the stunned Minotaur.

Oxar stood astonished for an age, staring at the consequence of his actions.

Swallowing, Oxar looked at the door and noticed a paper note beckoning him, he read it with a nod, and then he made his way to his new destination.

Chapter Nineteen
A Clever Cheat

Professor sat in front of her computer, rolling a pencil in between her finger tips, as green code sped across the screen, its light giving her eyes an emerald quality. Gronix had left her the vague, yet important, task of creating something to help her team win the game. He had hoped that she would create some sort of weapon, yet this was not the route Professor decided to go down. She believed that her R-Unit robotics had been a success, but they were too flawed for her liking. She had built nine R-Units since her arrival; two had been destroyed, three had become faulty, two had lost her signal and become subsequently lost in the island's wildlife, and whilst R3 still stood guard near her, she had heard reports of one of her creations 'jumping ship'. This betrayal was the final straw, and as such, Professor had decided to build her next breed of robotics: S-Unit.

Cannibalising the loose technology within the laboratory, Professor created a smaller, slimmer, sleeker model, making it faster and more agile than the previous eighteen models. Off of the original prototype, Professor reengineered her current assembly line, to manufactory the new line up, whilst she turned her attention to the computing technology; implementing multiple internal safeguards, with a constant connection with her wireless information distribution network.

R3 presented her with a cup of coffee when she relaxed in her chair, the advanced struggle finished. Smiling, she took the cup from the inferior machine, curious what it must be like to watch yourself become obsolete.

"Thank you, R3," Professor said, sipping the coffee, the delicious blend exactly as she had programmed it. Looking up at R3's red eyes, Professor's mind spiralled around the idea of upgrading this unit. Putting her cup down, she stood up, and began work on the obsolete R3 unit as her squad of S-Units were born on the ground floor.

***

Pandora woke lying on the cold throne room floor, her shut eyes providing a surface for images of her death to be projected upon.

"Pandora?" a friendly, electronic voice questioned, "Are you well?" Pandora frowned, and peeped through a single eye at the robotic face of R9 standing over her.

"R9?" Pandora asked, confused, "But you died..."

"As did you," R9 responded, "But I do understand your meaning." R9 offered her a metallic hand, with a sigh she accepted it, and was pulled to her feet.

"I assume we lost the overall encounter?" R9 pondered, an obvious disappointment lining its voice box.

"I'm not sure, I think Oxar had just defeated the other player, when Trigger killed the warlock," Pandora replied. "Come on, we should get back, Oxar may need our help." The pair stepped forward, activating a sensor.

"Hello there, R9," smiled Kaio, stepping into existence. R9 instantly readied himself for another confrontation, whilst Pandora just looked at their holographic kidnapper. "Welcome to *Eclipse*, to keep things interesting, I have decided to allow your addition to Team Solar, after Pandora corrupted your data banks, and gave you some form of 'free will'." R9 and Pandora shared a glance.

"As you may have noticed, I've already taken the liberty of installing a vanguard to your arm," Kaio said, pointing at R9's forearm, "It's more of an aesthetic issue than anything else. Anyway, allow me to formally and officially welcome you to Team Solar. You know the rules, good luck." With that Kaio faded into nothingness, and the pair were left alone in front of the large glowing revival crystal.

"Welcome to the team," Pandora said, breaking the silence.

"Thank you," R9 responded, before cocking his head to the side, "We need to leave."

***

R3 stood in front of Professor, her upgrades bulking the once slender machine, yet the power it now contained made Professor speculate if it could defeat the S-Units, that she had sent to each of the eight other capture locations on the island, with a single order; capture the flag, and keep hold of it.

Finishing her third cup of coffee, she hurled the cup into the air and clicked her tongue, activating R3's new weaponry system. Raising its arm, R3's wrist bent, exposing the barrel of one of Professor's experimental projectile weapons. As the cup reached the peak of its journey, the barrel made a soft click and the cup was frozen solid, smashing into a million pieces upon impact with the floor.

"Excellent!" Professor burst, clapping her hands slightly, "This deserves a re-titling; you are no longer R3." Professor grabbed a bottle off of her desk and dipped her finger into the black liquid.

Then, as she advanced, she continued, "You will now be XR." As she spoke, Professor wiped the black liquid over the R3 brand, the liquid melting into the metal, closing the brand's scar, and then with her forefinger, she dug the new name into its chest. XR was motionless throughout this interaction, its internal systems rewriting its main system file.

As Professor stepped back to admire her handiwork, the main laboratory doors burst open, and R9 and Pandora entered, the treacherous robot carrying the half-breed on its back.

"Welcome home, R9," Professor announced, looking down at them as Pandora dismounted. XR descended the stairs slowly, "And to what do I owe this pleasure?"

"Cut the bull," Pandora shouted. "We know your plan."

"Oh? And what's that? To win the game and put a stop to all this death?" Professor asked, "Is that the plan you're referring to?"

"Affirmative," R9 responded, looking up at its creator, "And your intention to reap the rewards, having never left this one location."

"And you two are going to stop me?" Professor

questioned, "A robotic traitor and… a half-elf." XR arrived at the bottom of the staircase.

"Excuse me, but I don't think so," Professor smiled venomously.

"And why's that?" Pandora asked, noticing XR advancing towards them.

"Because, of one word," Professor leaned on the banister, and whispered her contingency plan, "Dystopia."

"Dystopia?" Pandora repeated, "And what's that meant to do?" She looked around her, before she realised what the simple word had done. R9's upper torso had twisted round, and its left hand grabbed hold of Pandora's throat. Surprised, Pandora looked at her ally, but was met with the emotionless, red stare R9 had had when they had first met.

"R?" Pandora croaked, before pulling the Rip Jaw dagger out of her bag and driving it through R9's arm. R9 didn't react as Pandora yanked herself away from her friend, and R9's arm parted from its body and hung loosely around her neck.

"Come on R! Don't let her back in!" Pandora shouted, as XR reminded her of its presence, blasting the chair beside her with its freeze ray. Pandora yelped, as she stumbled into the solid object, that attached itself to her bottoms.

"You had fire, I'll give you that," Professor spoke kindly, XR passed the motionless R9, aiming at Pandora, who was cutting through her trouser fabric to get away from the immobilising chair. XR flipped a table out of its way as it neared its target. Pandora began to pant as she continued her endeavour in her helpless situation, slicing through the few remaining strands of material. Professor smirked then continued, "But in this game, brawn isn't everything."

"Affirmative," R9 chimed, plunging its right hand through XR's positronic brain.

"R9!" Pandora cheered, looking into its friendly green eyes once more. Professor roared in anger.

"No!" Professor screamed, "You will not use my own work against me!"

"Give up, lady," Pandora called, "You've lost, get over it."

"Lost?" Professor repeated weakly, before a small smile slipped onto her face, "But not everything."

Pandora frowned, before widening her eyes.

"R9, mute your hearing!" Pandora shouted, but as she did, Professor uttered the fateful word; "Boom." R9 twitched, dormant programs activating, electronic signals slicing through its freewill as they made their way to their destination.

"...R?" Pandora asked quietly, answered with a moments silence before R9 turned its face to Pandora.

"Thank you," R9 uttered, before the signals broke through the final self-preservation safe guard, and activated R9's self-destruction program.

R9's eyes went grey, its knees buckled, its body twitched furiously, and then R9 was motionless. Pandora stared at her friend; she had never watched something die in front of her. Even whilst on the island, something had distracted her view, sparing her of this overwhelming feeling. She wanted to simultaneously cry, and laugh, to remain motionless and to destroy everything in the room. Her mind raced, bouncing from emotion to emotion, unknowing of how to react.

"Well, that was anticlimactic," Professor smirked

and as if on cue, R9's head exploded, the chucks of metal hurling themselves across the room. A piece of R9's forehead shot across the distance between it and Pandora, the shrapnel sliced through her upper cheek. Professor cheered.

"That's better!" Professor chuckled, "A little more entertainment, before I remove you from this game." Pandora's eyes slowly rose to look up at the smirking creator, blood slowly leaking from her facial cut. Without a seconds thought, Pandora flicked her wrist, releasing the Rip Jaw dagger, it flew straight, and struck Professor's throat. Professor's eyes widened, blurring as her strength left her, and she slipped over the banister, the impact driving the blade deeper into her neck.

Pandora stood in silence, staring at the scene in front of her. After a moment, a large multiple-screened computer began to beep as the first S-Unit arrived at its location. Ascending the staircase, Pandora sat in front of the computer and began re-writing Professor's plan, wiping the DNA USB clean, and dabbing a drop of her blood onto it. Pandora smiled, hitting the accept button before returning to ground level.

Pandora retrieved her dagger. The computer shut down. Her vanguard updated, and Pandora left the Observatory, which had been captured for Team Solar, and headed for the final remaining capture point: Endless Falls.

Chapter Twenty
The Shooting Squads

Trigger sat by Endless Falls, a scrawled note crumpled in nir hand which read simply: 'T. Meet at top-right flag, P.' Ne had found it pinned to the grand doors of Sun Palace, next to another addressed to Oxar, when ne had awoken, nir body undamaged but nir gun cambers still empty. After reloading, Trigger had moved quickly to the rendezvous, waiting impatiently in the strangely relaxing environment. Ne sat on the north-east bank of the pool, staring across the water at the island view before nem. From nir seat, next to a water lodged S-Unit, ne could see the threatening volcano of Sun Palace, the distant shimmer of Run-Down Town, and the proud silhouette of Central Tower standing in front of the jagged tips of Famine Valley. Ne sighed as nir gaze drifted to the waterfall that rained from the sky, and fell into the clear waters before nir. Though clear, Trigger could scarcely make out the suspicious blurs of the dark blue and blood red creatures, which Kaio had informed nem were Kylocks, darting around in the water's depths.

Trigger swallowed as nir eyes returned to the mocking waving of the white flag that tormented nir view. Ne knew the dangers that Blue Crystal Island held, but even without them, the feat of capturing the flag would be too difficult for the skilled marksman. The natural ability to swim, tread water or even stay buoyant was lost on nem, the reason to learn the skill never presenting itself whilst in the sandy Riodic, or the timeless Vilderton; with its corrosive waters. As such, Trigger could only prepare nemself for whatever it was that Pandora had planned, and hope that nir inability was not an unforeseen hindrance.

As Trigger cleaned nir bolt-action repeating rifle, for the fifth time, ne heard the familiar stomps of nir teammate; Oxar. Looking through the rifle's scope, Trigger noticed that although he had recently been revived, his fur was covered in a strange black substance. As he neared, Trigger was still unseen by the Minotaur, a small bush provided nem with sufficient camouflage from onlookers. Instead of revealing nemself to him, Trigger chose to observe the beastly man, watching him as he approached the waters and dared to do what ne could not; Oxar dived into the pool, washing off the crusty, black substance before he began to swim towards the small island at its centre.

Approximately halfway between the bank and the island, Oxar dove under the surface, to Trigger this appeared to be merely an attempt to see what lurked beneath the surface. However, after a while his air bubbles began to surface alone, unaccompanied by the muscular mass, Trigger quickly realised that something was wrong. Abandoning nir position, Trigger dropped nir rifle opting for the quick barrage of bullets obtainable by nir trusted revolvers. Ne ran into the shallow waters of the bank and aimed across towards the last seen location of nir friend.

Oxar's screams were muffled by the warm waters that threatened to drown him, as small octopus-humanoid creatures latched on to his skin. Moving wildly, he had managed to hurl the first attacker away, but two more had grabbed him by the shoulders preventing him from resurfacing. Oxar looked down, and was instantly filled with a wish that he could un-see what waited below; twenty or more of the small water demons stood staring up at him, smiling widely with creepy toothless smirks and wide, unblinking eyes. Oxar dreaded to think what would happen if he was forced in to the creatures' grasps. As his scream bubbles broke on the surface, Oxar's vision began to blur, the octopus creatures dodging his heavy swings with ease as they continued to push him down.

A bullet burst through the rippling surface of the pool, the initial force of the round slowing dramatically as it tumbled through the water. Yet, it still hit its mark, and suddenly Oxar's left shoulder was no longer being submerged. Looking up at the remaining demon, he watched as it prepared its hind sword-like tentacles and readied itself to plunge them into Oxar's face, but before it could initiate its fatal attack, another round tumbled through the water and cut into its humanoid head.

Oxar rushed to the surface, hungrily welcoming the cold air into his lungs before swimming as quickly as he could back to the bank. The pair of deceased Kylocks drifted down to their brethren, who reacted accordingly, when fresh meat falls into the laps of hungry monsters.

***

The Blue Revival Crystal of Nocturnal Castle shone brightly in front of the metallic figure of S-Unit 1. Professor breathed in deeply as the coding of her being finished, and the soothing light was reduced to nothingness once more. Professor stared up to at the bright sky, darkening as the sun began its descent.

"Well, that was an unforeseen turn of events," Professor mumbled to herself, lifting her glasses momentarily to rub her tired eyes. Sitting up, Professor looked over her new environment, the infamous 'Nocturnal Castle' that had presented itself on her vanguard only a number of hours ago, yet the time had felt like days to her. Her gaze rested on one of her latest creations, the smooth, slender body of her newest robotic design, the S-Unit stared back. Professor's face crumpled into a frown as she realised that her eyes were not being met with the electronic silver that she had programmed them with, but instead she was greeted with a pair of strangely familiar emerald eyes.

Her own eyes widened as she remembered where she had seen those kind of eyes before, the way the edges danced as new, corrupt coding battled with its starting programs. Yet, Professor had no time to react to this knowledge. The S-unit had already pierced her chest before her vision could catch up. Blood gushed out of her mouth, and her mind clung to one conclusion; she had been successful in making her creations faster.

Professor fell back, as the S-Unit approached the dark blue flag, with a cream moon symbol in the centre. It stretched out its long, thin fingers, its fingertips turning green where it should have fingerprints, and in one clean motion, the S-Unit grabbed hold of the flag, and it burst into the rich yellow and red of its new master's colours.

***

Pandora smiled as her vanguard beeped, but she didn't slow her pace to look at it. She knew what the vanguard had to say and instead chose to continue running. Her heartbeat pounded in her ears, her blood burnt in her veins, her body screamed for stillness but she didn't slow her pace. She couldn't slow her pace.

***

Gronix and Murados had passed Central Tower when their vanguards beeped viciously at them, notifying the pair of the sudden change. Murados stopped in her tracks, Gronix's cloak blowing in the wind around her, but it held fast, clinging loosely to her body.

"What the Zxaperia?" she roared, looking at the beeping contraption. Gronix couldn't reply; his jaw was firmly clenched as he stared unblinkingly at his own vanguard.

"This is…" he began, before words failed him and he let out a monstrous roar. With a simple utterance, Gronix hurled a tornado of flame towards the wooden town that had appeared on the horizon.

The pair stared as the fire engulfed the town.

"There's only one flag left," Murados stated, looking at her wrist, "that's where they'll be heading."

"Then let's make sure, we don't make it easy for them," Gronix said, his eyes reflecting the flames, "I... do not... lose."

***

Oxar sat on the bank opposite Trigger; they had spoken and decided that this would be the best course of action. Oxar dropped another small stone into the clear waters and watched it sink out of sight, the Kylocks' movements informing him an approximate landing location. When he looked over at his teammate, he could scarcely make out the shadowy form hidden within the small poolside shrubbery.

He knew what would happen next, and the consequences of his actions back in Sun Palace, but he could not find the words to talk about it. He was the one that suggested the partition, worried that if he stood near Trigger too long, he would confess his fears of what will happen next. He had not experienced the effects of a revival crystal before, but even without a degree in science or mana, he was fairly sure that the crumbled ruins at Sun Palace would not be reviving anything any time soon.

If he fell in this battle, Oxar doubted he would fight in another.

As his mind continued to throw itself around the possibilities of what could be, he felt a sudden burst of heat behind him as Run-Down Town caught ablaze.

It wouldn't be long now.

The shooting squad would soon arrive, and meet with his own murderous lot.

At least they had chosen a pretty place for Death to visit.

Chapter Twenty-One
Casualties

Trigger saw them first, the two specks on the horizon, the flames casting harsh orange light over their bodies as they marched towards Endless Falls. Ne smiled, considering how easy they had made it for nem. Lining up the shot, Trigger got the female warlock figure of Murados in the centre of nir crosshairs, and then adjusting for distance and wind, ne pulled the trigger.

Previously unseen Woboks burst out of a nearby tree, disturbed by the sudden explosion of sound. Trigger lowered nir rifle, reloading whilst ne looked out across the horizon, and acknowledged that only a lone figure now strolled towards the pool. Ne licked nir lips as the fresh round was locked into the chamber, the metallic click almost covering the snap of a twig to nir left.

Trigger turned quickly, raising nir rifle at the threat, but the barrel was caught by nir assailant, who stood before nem wearing a thin, black cloak and a bloodthirsty expression. Murados smiled cruelly as she watched a flicker of annoyance cross Trigger's face, she leaned forwards grabbing hold of the front Trigger's jacket.

"It's not nice to shoot at monsters," Murados said.

Trigger grabbed her hand, as Murados uttered, "Pyroska!"

Trigger's clothes burst into flames, scorching nir exposed flesh in a heartbeat. Trigger screamed, nir skin crisping as the hot air around nem became thick with smoke, yet through the pain and noise, ne could hear the cackling of nir attacker. Murados had released Trigger, wanting an unobstructed view of her victim burning alive; a mistake. As strength began to leave nem, Trigger raised nir arms; the rifle still clung tightly in nir hands, and pulled the trigger. The bullet smashed into Murados' unprepared stomach, sending her flying into the pool, and down into the welcoming tentacles of the Kylocks below.

Trigger dropped nir rifle, and stumbled towards the water. Beyond the crackling flames, ne could hear Oxar fighting and Pandora calling to nem. Ne fell to nir knees on the pool's bank, the heat absorbing all the moisture from nir being, as ne wanted to cry through the pain. Trigger rocked back and forth on the edge of awareness, and then the heat caused even more damage to nem.

One by one, the flames licked the shells Trigger had wrapped around nir person, and one by one the gun powder within each round exploded. Bullets shot in every direction, many hurtling across the pool, some flying off towards Kaio Mansion behind nem, and a few turning against their previous owner, slicing through Trigger's flesh.

Trigger fell forward into the water, the liquid instantly putting out the flames, cooling nir burns but also stopping nir blood from clotting. Trigger stared down at the Kylocks dancing around Murados, tearing her flesh to pieces, as ne lay in the shallow waters, the waves rolled nem onto nir front as the world before nir eyes brightened, and nir life began to flash before nem.

***

Pandora had seen the distant Run-Down Town be consumed by a fiery hurricane, the orange glow casting vicious shadows on the world. She identified two of the shadows that marched away from her as two of Team Nocturnal's heavy hitters. Pandora didn't let up her pace, her muscles had long since grown tired of screaming for her to stop and now ached quietly, as her father's elven genes kept her tired body moving.

She heard a gunshot, and watched one of the pair flash out of existence as the bullet smashed harmlessly into the ground. The pool of water came into view and Pandora could make out Oxar's strong silhouette against the reflective pool, Gronix marching towards the Minotaur with curled fists, and two figures on the other side of the water.

Pandora watched Oxar breathe fire towards the approaching warlock, who retaliated by turning the oxygen around Oxar's head into a poisonous blue gas. Oxar's eyes widened as his lungs shutdown, attempting to cut off his supply of toxic air. Gronix chuckled as Oxar moved wildly, swinging his arm frantically as he attempted to disperse the cloud that clung to his face. Charging forward, Pandora unsheathed the Rip Jaw dagger and drove it into Gronix's right shoulder. Gronix roared, the cloud dispersed, Oxar fell to his knees gasping deeply, praying that the damage to his lungs was minimal, and Pandora situated herself between her weakened teammate and the wounded warlock, as adrenaline pumped through her system reviving her aching muscles.

"Three against two? Hardly fair," Gronix breathed out slowly, his hand covering his wound, his skin knitting back together. Then, Gronix brought his blooded hand to his lips. Pandora pressed forward, knowing better than to let the warlock finish his incantation, and made to drive her blade into Gronix's chest. Yet, her movements were too slow, with the incantation complete, Gronix opened his bloody palm towards her, and a black hand erupted out of the dark red fluid, catching her dagger. Gronix smiled, pulling his hand away from her, while the dark hand clung tightly to the blade. The blood stretched out across the distance, drooping as it formed the familiar nightmarish structure of the demon: Omiss.

Omiss stared into the fearful eyes of Pandora, snapping the Rip Jaw blade between his fingers, with a smile. Pandora fell back, clutching the hilt firmly, as the demon kept its eerie eye contact, advancing slowly on the disarmed hybrid. As he drew closer, Omiss began to reach out towards his next meal, but was momentarily distracted by the strange material that had been wrapped around his forearm. Suddenly, a cloud of fire smashed into the demon, lighting its dark flesh ablaze as the flames cocooned it. Omiss grabbed his left shoulder and tore off his top layer of fiery skin, before turning his attention to the weakened Minotaur that had attempted to attack him.

"You," Omiss breathed, his smile growing crueller, "We shall play again, now, but I will not be a nice as I once was." Omiss moved slowly over to Oxar, whose body shook as his mind recalled all the false memories

Omiss had made him live. The demon reached out his long, blackened fingers to Oxar's face, but halted when he heard his summoner yell.

"No!" Gronix yelled, as Pandora plunged the remains of the blade into a scroll with a crudely drawn circle, within which was the Zxaperian symbol of 'return'. Omiss scowled as he watched his own blood roll down the blade and soak the centre of the circle, the scroll turned black as the circle unravelled into satanic tendrils, opening a small hole back into the Nightmare Plains, from which he was summoned. Omiss couldn't move as the tendrils blindly detected their demonic target and grabbed hold of him, wrapping themselves around his newly resurrected form before they proceeded to drag him back to his own realm. Within moments Gronix stood without his demonic pet.

"You, scum!" Gronix roared, his fists unclenching as he readied himself to destroy the girl who had banished Omiss, but as he did, another gunshot diverted his attention to across the pond. Gronix watched as a body fell into the water and sank, and a figure of fire stood swaying, the flames engulfing their victim.

"Trigger!" Pandora screamed, glancing over to what had distracted the warlock. This was his chance, Gronix raised his left hand, but Oxar pushed Pandora out of the way, and was caught in Gronix's grasp, the Minotaur's eyes widened as he lost another ability to the warlock. Gronix bared his teeth, annoyed by the switch, but not stopping his bloodthirsty actions, as he struggled to raise his right hand. Pandora darted in front of him and, with the few centimetres of blade that remained on the Rip Jaw dagger hilt, sliced through his throat.

Gronix swayed, dropping the Minotaur, his attention

returning to the girl, his strength pouring out of him, he grabbed her throat with his left hand, turning away from the pool as he forced his fingers to apply more pressure.

"I... will... not... lose," Gronix mumbled between pained breaths. Across the water, there was an explosion. Pandora watched as her burning friend's body convulsed as every shell on nir person exploded. Pandora grabbed hold of Gronix's arm and pulled herself against him. Gronix began to object to this movement, but suddenly it didn't matter. The improper firing and distance had slowed the rounds, but they still burrowed into their impact spots. Gronix stood motionless, as silence fell over the landscape. When Pandora released him, Gronix desired to attack her, to have revenge for what had happened, but as he tried to step forwards, his legs collapsed beneath him, and his blurred vision was consumed with grass and mud.

Pandora stood over the warlock for a few moments, his back covered in bloody entrance wounds, the blood seeping into his shirt as his life leaked out of his body. A splash across the water brought her back to reality.

Quickly, she darted over to her fallen comrade. Oxar's chin was covered in blood, his breathing was deep and struggling; the poison had caused sufficient damage to achieve its desire, and the leaking bullet wounds in his torso told her that death was inevitable. Pandora took his face in her hands, and braved a smile.

"It's okay," she whispered, "It'll all be okay, just let it happen, and I'll see you real soon, okay?" It was then when she noticed the fear filled tears that stained the Minotaur's cheeks.

"No," he replied, "The demon... I... the revival crystal, it's bust... this is it." Pandora stared at him speechless, as his words slowly sunk in. She pulled him close, and as his struggle to breathe worsened, tears began to roll down her cheeks.

"I, I didn't, want to, to play," he stuttered, "I, I want to, to go home." Then the struggle became too great, ever breath became shallower, and then his lungs completely shut down. Pandora sat there in silence as Oxar's body went still in her arms, her tears wetting the Minotaur's fur.

***

"Hey beautiful," Pandora said quietly as she pulled Trigger to the bank. Nir exposed skin was blistered, nir goggles were full of water and nir neckerchief was burnt to a thin, stringy lace of fabric covering a reddened lower face. Carefully, Pandora removed nir goggles.

"Hey," Trigger replied, nir voice barely a whisper, "Great plan." Ne smiled weakly, before instantly grimacing.

"I ... I didn't think this..." Pandora began quietly, her mind dwindling on how she was once again helpless to help her dying friend.

"I know," Trigger looked up at the waterfall, "It'll be okay." Pandora could see through Trigger's bluff, but the words were comforting to hear.

"How?" Pandora asked softly, "How are you so strong?" Trigger's gaze lowered to Pandora's face.

"Well, one of us had to be," Trigger smiled again, "And you didn't give me much choice, being the pretty one, an' all." Pandora let out a short chuckle, before her emotions caught up with her.

"Promise me," Trigger began, staring into Pandora's

eyes, "Promise me, you'll win."

Pandora nodded. "I promise."

Overcome with emotion, she leant down and kissed the dying gunslinger softly on the lips.

"It's been fun," Trigger whispered as their lips parted.

***

Pandora stood up, picking up Trigger's blood-soaked revolver and fired it at the flag. As Trigger's blood smacked into it, the flag changed into the once comforting rising sun. As Pandora looked at it, she gained no comfort from the image.

Breathing deeply, she readied herself.

Turning on the spot, she looked at her next destination: Kaio Mansion.

Chapter Twenty-Two
Violent Peace

Kaio sat on a small hill, upon a pile of autumn leaves beneath a leafless tree, staring out across Grothaig. He had always loved this country, ever since his father had brought him here when he was only a few years old, to this exact spot. The memory had been etched into his mind, and though time had blurred the specifics, he still held on to the imagery fondly.

"Commander Kaio," a nearby voice called, "Your team is ready on your mark." Kaio didn't look over; instead he focused on the shimmering light of a distant lake that wormed its way through the trees. His eyes followed the lake, and fell upon a pack of Grimalkin drinking deeply in a small clearing. Why had such a peaceful, beautiful place been chosen for this war?

"Commander Kaio?" the voice asked, drawing nearer, "Kaio? Are you well?" With a sigh, Kaio looked over to his brother-in-arms.

"I was, Rinast, before your face destroyed this view," Kaio smirked, as his tall, blonde friend feigned insult. He and Rinast Higlo had joined the Borantik forces at the same time, and though they had been placed in multiple different platoons since their first meeting, fate had decided to reunite them on the battlefield.

"You and your views," Rinast chuckled, "Remember back in Henthaa, when you found that clearing with the Yiraks? What was that place called?"

"Frostgotten Crest," Kaio answered with a smile, "I wanted to set up camp for a few hours, stop and smell the ruben's, but you wanted to finish the mission and get home." Rinast nodded, chuckling as he remembered the next part of the story.

"And then Archie caught up, and yelled at us for arguing, and one of the Yiraks heard him shouting and chased him round the clearing for an hour!" Rinast laughed.

"I swear, if he wasn't an arachne, he would have gotten an antler in the arse," Kaio chuckled. The pair stared out at the view for a few moments, reminiscing on old times but slowly their chuckles died away and the reality of their situation resurfaced.

"How's the wife?" Rinast queried, as silence fell between them.

"Merkas?" Kaio asked rhetorically, only saying it aloud to hear her name once more, "Yeah, she says she's okay. Her last letter said she's given birth…"

"You old dog," Rinast smiled, "You never even said she was pregnant."

"Well, you know me, Rin," Kaio answered, looking up at his friend, "I wouldn't say my own name if it didn't come up in conversation." Rinast chuckled.

"Come on then, what's the kid's name?" He asked, wanting to keep the conversation going for as long as possible, desperately holding on to this moment of calm, before they had to return to the terror he knew would unfold soon enough.

"Firyos, a little girl," Kaio smiled, looking back out across the scene, "And I'm out here, knocking on Death's door."

"Come on, don't think like that," Rinast said, sitting beside Kaio, "You'll be fine, I'll be fine, we'll all be fine. Come tomorrow, this will all be over. I've heard the higher-ups talking about some new weapon, or spell they've cooked up. They say it's going to turn the tables and end the war, in one sweep."

The two sat in silence, Rinast pondered the power of this 'thing' that was meant to end their fight, while Kaio's thought remained on what he had had to leave behind when the war started.

"Look," Rinast began, "I get it, I've always understood, but I get it now, and the simple fact is people need violence. They need to feel threatened, terrified, and horrified by what others can do… we're a means to an end. We don't want to be here, and I'm pretty sure the people we're fighting don't want to be here either, but some group of people high up on both sides; they love this. I wouldn't be surprised if they weren't recording our fights and jacking off in some underground bunker. When this weapon gets here; that'll be the people spent, all that pent up aggression, anger, blood-lust… it'll be gone and we'll be in peace, just you watch. And after that happens, we can meet up and have a beer, and we'll laugh about how you were sat on the top of some hill like a scared kid."

They both smiled at this plausible future, as a gunshot went off nearby, the echo ricocheting off of every tree until it disturbed the drinking Grimalkin in the clearing. The Grimalkin pack, looked out, their ears prepared for another sound, but hearing none, they chose to skulk back into the tree line. Kaio watched them with a sinking heart.

"It's called Hellfire," Kaio stated, getting up, "The weapon, they've been working on. It's a mana bomb; they're going to activate it in the centre of the country, at the rise of blood moon. It's going to set the land on fire, everything will burn, and the chance of anything surviving is... Take my advice, Rin: tell who you can, then get out of here."

"That would be breaking rank," Rinast stated, getting to his feet, "And they wouldn't just bomb the place without pulling us out first."

"What we've done here; what's all been for? Peace? Justice? Open your eyes Rinast, you said it yourself, people need violence, and we're here because someone decided they didn't like Grothaig's flag. Do you think they want the people at home to know that? Do you think that's a good enough excuse for all this violence?"

Kaio couldn't look at Rinast as he finished what he needed to say, "I'm taking my team to the shore, I'm planting a Borantik flag into the sand; completing my orders, and then I'm taking myself, my team and any innocents that I can get my hands on, and I'm high-tailing off this island before it turns into a death trap. I advise you do the same." With that, Kaio turned on his heels and left Rinast under the leafless tree, contemplating his purpose in Grothaig, why he had joined the forces, and what he would do next.

***

Kaio thumbed his palm, tracing the pale scar line that served as a constant reminder of his time in Grothaig. He was sat at the top of the grand hall staircase, waiting for this season's champion to claim her prize. He had assumed the position sixteen times before, and had fallen into a nice groove when it came to the end of his 'game'.

The door handle rattled as someone outside grabbed hold of it, Kaio looked up but chose not to move. The door burst open, and five bullets smashed into the wall above Kaio's head. Pandora stood in the doorway, a revolver in her hand, the smoking barrel aimed slightly above the seated Kaio.

"Nice of you to join," Kaio stated, putting his foot onto a lower step, and then pushing himself up, creating a seamless movement as he began his descent to the ground floor. Pandora adjusted her aim, and fired her final shot. The bullet hurtled towards Kaio, but he merely whipped his hand across his chest and the bullet transformed into sand, harmlessly pummelling his shirt.

"Are you quite finished?" Kaio asked, as Pandora pulled the trigger again, and heard the harmless click as the hammer fell onto an empty chamber.

"Put it down," Kaio encouraged, "This is a time of celebration, not aggression. You won!" He smiled widely, raising his hands to activate trumpet sounds and a hail of balloons to fall from the ceiling. Pandora didn't react to his showmanship, staring at the 'God' and seeing only a monster in a black and red suit.

Kaio sighed as his gaze fell back onto his victor.

"Nothing? You know, the others smiled at least..." Kaio started, "Oh... I understand... You're like everyone else, huh? You're pinning me as the bad guy." Kaio nodded, striding down the last few steps.

"That makes sense," Kaio stopped in front of Pandora, "I am the one that brought you here, made you fight for your life, made you kill people, made others kill you, and now you're alone. Once a thief with a clean conscious, and now you're a murderer, ready to kill me sooner than look at me. I get it; I'm the bad guy in your eyes." Kaio smiled.

"And that's fine, because I don't need you to like me," Kaio stated, "I only need you to produce view-worthy content, and you did that by the barrel. But, we don't have to end here."

"What?" Pandora asked, as the words conjured more bloodshed in her mind.

"Well, you are the winner," Kaio smiled, "You can have your prize and walk away, quite literally, you could leave here with a clean slate and more money than you could ever spend; no criminal record, no ties holding you down, just you and an endless bank account, just what you've always dreamt of... but I wouldn't be a very good entertainer if I didn't provide an ultimatum."

Pandora's breathing softened as she considered a crime-free life, where she could do as she pleased within the law. She could walk down main roads without fear of flashing lights, she wouldn't have to run whenever she saw a police officer, and she would be able to travel freely, see the sights, visit her brother in Riodic, explore Vilderton...

"I don't mean to interrupt," Kaio said, ripping Pandora out of her fantasy world, "But, I will need an answer eventually, I mean, I can add in a dramatic pause post-production, but right now, I'm on a bit of a schedule."

"What?" Pandora said, "What answer?"

"Well, it wouldn't be your decision if it was my answer, would it?" Kaio smiled, "Do you want to take your prize and leave? Or do you want to gamble and try to save some lives?"

"What do you mean?" Pandora frowned, "Gamble how?"

"Well, it wouldn't be a gamble, if you knew all the details," Kaio smiled, the room darkening as unseen spotlights lit up the pair, providing the camera pods with a very dramatic scene.

"Run or Gamble? Your life or Multiple?" Kaio asked, "Only you can decide."

Pandora swallowed, looking down at the empty revolver in her hand.

She nodded, and then slowly looked up at Kaio.

"I'll gamble," She stated.

Kaio nodded, taking out a small red crystal from his inside breast pocket and then threw it into the air.

There was a flash of red light that illuminated the room, the glow making Pandora feel rejuvenated, the revolver felt heavier as it loaded itself, and then she realised that she was surrounded by all those who had fallen in the game.

"Good choice," Kaio smiled.

Chapter Twenty-Three
Victory

With a click of his fingers, Kaio disappeared, reappearing at the top of the stairs, and looking down on the ten players of the game. He watched them all look at each other unknowing of what was happening, all but Pandora who stared coldly at the self-named God.

"Welcome back," Kaio shouted, "How was temporary death?" He smiled as all the players stopped looking at each other, and turned their attention to him. They all slowly realised that the Limbo they had been locked within, was merely a plain of existence by Kaio's creation.

"Through the generous act of Pandora, you have all been resurrected for one last chance of success," Kaio stated. "However, be warned, this is the last time. No more freebies." Kaio paused, allowing the silence to engulf them all as his words washed over them.

"For interesting content, people would say I should only allow one person or one team to win, but I've done that before, and it was boring," Kaio continued, looking at each of their faces. "So! I'm going to provide you with an opportunity for five, and only five, players to win. Understood?" The ten players made a soft ramble, they knew that they had no choice in the matter, and had learnt that defying the rules would only cause them to be ripped out of existence once more.

"Good," Kaio smiled, "The new game is a little simpler than the last; I will be bringing five copies of my son, Champ, into the room, whoever kills a copy, saves their own life, leaving the other five players to their final resting places. Every man, woman and Trigger for themselves." Kaio smirked, rubbing his hands together.

"Good luck," Kaio finished, separating his palms before smacking them together for a single, loud clap. The clap reverberated off of the stone walls of the grand entrance hall, and five Champs rose through the five circular, coloured floor tiles that skirted the ten players; red, blue, green, yellow and purple. Once the echo of the clap had faded, returning to an imperfect silence, the Champs attacked.

The Yellow Champ was the first to land his attack, grabbing hold of the back of Professor's head and pulling her below his mouth. He roared fire into the ill prepared Professor's, spectacle wearing, face. Professor screamed, allowing the flames to crawl down her throat and cook her from within. In mere seconds, Yellow Champ dropped the roasted woman to the ground, and began eyeing up his next target.

Pandora moved quickly, slipping between Oxar and a female harkall as the Purple Champ made to grab hold of her.

"Trigger!" she called, as the gunslinger punched the Green Champ in the mouth, silencing his fiery attack, and temporarily dazing the creature. Trigger looked over to Pandora, and caught the white handle of the now fully-loaded, black revolver that she had tossed to nem.

Trigger smiled at Pandora, and for a moment the battlefield quietened around them, but only for a moment. The Green Champ was no longer dazed, and had grabbed Triggers shoulder.

"It would appear you are in need of assistance," R9 stated from beside Trigger. Before ne could object, R9 had punched Green Champ in the face, dispatching this incarnation of Champ as he had the one back in Central Tower. In the blink of an eye R9 disappeared, and reappeared beside Kaio, under a small, green spotlight. A trumpet sounded, letting the fighters know that one fighter had been successful.

Omiss refused to fail another task, it had only been a few seconds in Vanicrast, but in the moments before Kaio had transported Omiss from Zxaperia to his Limbo, Lord Termin had reminded him what failure does to a demon. Omiss watched the tall, grey-haired man, dressed in a yellow waistcoat and jeans, burn his ex-teammate to a smouldering crisp, and realised that Kaio had not tipped the scales in the players favour. Omiss glanced to his left, and saw the unfamiliar figure of Almar. She wore a Nocturnal vanguard, but they had never met this strange winged player before. Omiss smiled, and grabbed hold of her wrist, instantly she attempted to retaliate, but she was unfamiliar to his ways, and in seconds Omiss had absorbed himself into her form. From within, Omiss smacked Almar's soul off of the controls and took temporary ownership of this winged life form.

Almar and Oxar stood in front of a Champ dressed in purple, whose burnt wings kept him hovering slightly above the ground. Oxar moved first, driving his fist into the man's stomach, but Omiss refused to allow the

Minotaur to get the kill. Almar's body shot forward, her hand grabbed hold of Champs throat and the two sped up to the ceiling, leaving Oxar grounded. Champ grabbed hold of Almar's wrist his body in spasm as he unsuccessfully attempted to throw off Almar's attack. Omiss smiled from within Almar's body, and then drove Almar and the Purple Champ hurtling into the ground.

Purple Champ's neck broke on impact, shattering floor tiles and killing him instantly. A trumpet sounded, as Almar was returned control of her body, a moment before she would have smashed into the stone floor too. Omiss floated on Kaio's right, a purple spotlight exaggerating his darker qualities as he smiled widely down at the remaining fighters.

Oxar had watched in annoyance as the harkall and Purple Champ shot up into the air, but he was quickly given another objective to focus on, as Kors punched Oxar in the face.

"Brawlax!" Kors roared, "I'll kill you for what you've done to my people!" Oxar looked at the aquatican in confusion.

"What?" Oxar replied, as he watched Kors pull out a pair of Rip Jaw teeth from his lower back scales, "Who even are you?"

"I am Kors!" he shouted in return, ignoring the fighting around them as he focused solely on the Minotaur, "Soldier of Ingswa! And King Raddis will erect a statue of my likeness when he hears of how I have slain you."

"But I'm…" Oxar started, but the aquatican refused to hear, believing that Oxar was the infamous, Minotaur warlord of Grothaig, Lord Brawlax. Kors moved quickly, darting across the short distance between the two fighters, and swung the two and a half inch blades at the confused Minotaur.

Gronix muttered his favourite spell as he raised his hand towards the Red son of Kaio, a purple, empty spiral appeared out of thin air directly behind Champ's spine; he smiled as the spiral tried to latch onto his clothes, but then they were smacked away by the genes he inherited from his father.

Murados watched the spell rebound off of the Red Champ, and smirked as she planned her next move. Charging forward, Murados barged into Gronix's back, rolling past the warlock and grabbing hold of Champ. Champ scowled, grabbing hold of Murados's wrists, but his efforts were fruitless as Murados buried her teeth into Champ's arm, tearing into his pale skin. Blood sprayed across her face as she swallowed Champ's flesh. The transformation began instantly, black feathered wings burst through her shoulder blades, tearing through the cloak Gronix had unwillingly given her.

Gronix regained his footing as Champ pushed the winged form of Murados away from him.

"I should have killed you a long time ago," Gronix roared as he hurled a ball of fire at the shape-shifter. The flames bent around her as the spell dispersed, its effects nullified. The fire licked her cloak as she looked back at the angry warlock.

"I couldn't agree more," Murados smiled, grabbing hold of Gronix's face and picking him up, "Goodbye little warlock." Bringing her fingers together, Murados buried her nails into his screaming face. A loud crack went unheard in the battlefield, the noise engulfed by yelling and the smash of floor tiles. Yet, to one person, the crack was a death sentence, as bone fractured and punctured, tearing ligaments and destroying muscle tissue. Gronix fell to the ground, a lifeless doll on a board of players.

A trumpet sounded after Murados turned her attention to the Red Champ, and tore through his body, adding another kill to the pile of bodies she left in her wake.

Oxar caught Kors's hands as they descended towards his chest, he knew that there was little point arguing with the aquatican, as nothing would change if he managed to persuade Kors, as they would still end up fighting to the death in Kaio's game. Instead, Oxar lifted Kors by the wrists and smashed his horned forehead into his opponent's undefended face, shattering Kors's nose. Blood burst out of his nose, covering Oxar's face, but this did not deter the Minotaur as he head-butted the aquatican again, splattering blood across them both. Kors's eyes blurred as he watched Oxar smash into his face for a third time. After the fourth, Kors dropped his Rip Jaw teeth, and after the fifth, Kors had lost consciousness.

Oxar hurled the unconscious Kors at the Blue Champ, who had been throwing punches at the agile Pandora. Kors's body provided Pandora with the opportunity to roll away from her attacker. Oxar stepped over the rolling Pandora and punched Blue Champ in the face.

Mid-roll, Pandora picked up the dropped Rip Jaw teeth, smiling as she jumped back up onto her feet, and quickly glanced at the shanks in her hands. Pandora revelled in the simplicity of her new aquatican weaponry, but her appreciation was short lived as the Yellow Champ grabbed her shoulder. Moving quickly,

Pandora plunged one of the teeth into the Champ's hand, spinning around and slashing the other tooth across Champ's throat. The Champ in yellow fell forward, his knees smashing into the floor tiles, his hands clutching his throat as blood seeped between his fingers. Pandora looked into his eyes, regretting her actions for just a moment, before smashing the tooth into Champ's left eye, driving it in as deep as possible. A trumpet sounded.

Oxar threw the Blue Champ into the centre of the room, surrounded by the remaining survivors of the new game; Almar clicked her wrist and Trigger rolled the revolver cylinder across nir outer thigh.

"Sudden death," Kaio murmured with a smile, as he allowed the camera pods to come out of hiding and film in the open. Pandora's face fell as she realised that only one of her teammates could survive. She struggled against an invisible force, within the yellow lighting, that held her fixed to her place at the top of the stairs.

Oxar advanced on the final Champ, Trigger aimed, yet Almar moved first; hurtling forwards and grabbing hold of Champ's blue waistcoat, before she rocketed up towards the ceiling. Oxar's eyes widened as they soared up out of his reach. Trigger raised nir revolver, and fired twice, the bullets severing Almar's muscle tissue attaching her wings to her torso. The pair fell, hurtling towards the ground, as the two were powerless against the forces of gravity.

Almar hit the ground first, blood exploding from her mouth as her neck collided with the floor. Champ, however, remembered the skinned wings that plastered his back and moments before impact, Champ halted his descent. Champ smirked as he looked down at the bloody harkall corpse.

Oxar tackled Champ out of the air, and the pair slammed into one of the stone pillars that held up the balcony above them. Oxar landed softly, holding a limp Champ in his hands. A trumpet sounded, Oxar looked at Trigger as he disappeared, while Trigger gave an encouraging smile, before turning to face Kaio.

"You have performed well, Trigger," Kaio announced, "But a God must stick to his word, else man will not believe in his power, or his plan. Good night, Gunslinger."

"Fuck you," Trigger smiled, as Kaio clicked his fingers and nir figure was embraced in Death's lace, the lace slithered across nir body, then tore through nir flesh and reduced nem to a pile of red mulch, to the music of Pandora's screams for mercy.

***

Kaio stood in front of the five winners of *Eclipse*, each on the coloured circle of the respective Champ they dispatched.

"Oxar," Kaio began, "Born a prince, self-exiled as a monster, proven on the battlefield as a warrior. I have seen into your heart, and will grant your wish." Oxar opened and shut his mouth like a fish out of water, as Kaio placed his hand on Oxar's forehead, between his horns and whispered the words to cure his Minotaur curse. In mere moments, Oxar's furred flesh moulted revealing his original human form. When the spell was complete, Oxar fell to his knees and wept as he stared at his pale, human hands. Kaio advanced to the neighbouring purple and green circles.

"R9, Omiss," Kaio smiled, addressing them each in

turn, "You were brought into the game without my input, and although you have been granted the privilege of being official players within the game, I have not seen into your hearts. What is it that you desire?"

"My desire?" R9 repeated, "I have found this experience rewarding, and I do not wish to leave. My desire is to become a permanent addition to *Eclipse*, and to learn more of what I can now do." Kaio raised an eyebrow, before nodding.

"Very well," Kaio replied, "You may have full access to all the scientific technologies at my disposal. And for you, Omiss?" Omiss frowned, and bared his teeth.

"Ah, yes," Kaio smiled, "I understand. Consider it done." With a click of his fingers the thick red-ringed pattern around his wrists dissolved into his red and black skin, his lower torso sealed and grew, gifting him with two lower extremities to stand upon, and a black loin cloth that covered his new formed privates. Kaio continued to walk around to Murados, in the red circle.

"Miranda Sty," Kaio said, stopping in front of her, "I will give you what you desire, and more." Kaio placed his hand upon her head, and whispered the words of cure once more. Murados's eyes widened, as her memories returned; her life before the operation, the experimental operation to cure her illness, the paperwork that confirmed that they weren't trying to cure her at all, and the doctor's gasps as the injected fluids had their desired effects before stopping her heart.

"Memories and control," Kaio confirmed, "From now on, the forms you 'sample', you will always be able to access." Kaio then finished the circle, arriving in front of Pandora.

"Last but not least?" Pandora enquired, smiling as she wiped her moist cheeks.

"Exactly," Kaio answered, "I have already wiped away your criminal record and your bank account has been attached to another that will constantly refill it, so if you'd accepted my original offer, we would be settled." Pandora frowned slightly, confused by Kaio's words.

"But you gambled. So, I have one more prize for you," Kaio stated, loving this part of the game.

Chapter Twenty-Four
Game Over

Omiss sat atop a chapel steeple, rubbing his aching legs. The realm of Vanicrast had always seemed so small to him when he was bound to Zxaperia, but now that he got to experience it, the small world seemed to have grown around him. Everyday Omiss would find new things that puzzled and confused him, new places to search and new lands to discover but even though he knew that he had more than enough time to explore, he always found himself sprinting from one place to another. He had been worried at first, his appearance being so different, but from the first day his skin went by unnoticed, his uneasy steps never questioned, and his sharpened teeth were treated with the same inconspicuousness. He blended effortlessly into the peculiarities of Vanicrast, just another mystery left to its own devices until it caused a problem.

"Omiss," a female voice called, "Would you get down already? I thought we were going for food." Omiss smiled once more at the view, he was now free to explore all he wanted. He looked up at the night sky and laughed, he was surrounded by beauty, by innocence, and by monsters. He felt at home; fearless, happy, comforted.

"Omiss?" The warlock girl below called again, "Come on, I'm starving!"

"I'm coming, Melody," Omiss smiled, "Just a moment."

Little Melody Able had grown into a beautiful, intellectual woman, who had followed in her father's footsteps and became a high standing lawyer. One night, after she had settled in front of her television, her thick, curly, red hair attempting to escape a loose ponytail, and tub of low-fat ice cream in her lap, she had seen her childhood friend.

Omiss had heard her try to summon him whilst on Gronix's leash, and again after he'd been freed. With his newfound freedom, he decided to join his old acquaintance, and the two became fast friends.

Omiss leapt from the steeple and landed beside Melody. At first she was startled, always forgetting his theatrical abilities, but her shock was soon replaced by joy as he took her in his arms.

"Just a moment," Omiss whispered, pulling her close and breathing her in as if for the first time once more. Melody smiled, wrapping her arms around his neck.

"I guess, one more moment wouldn't hurt," Melody replied. Omiss smiled sweetly, and pressed his mouth against hers.

Vanicrast had always been so interesting to Omiss, but Melody had grown into the most beautiful thing in the realm.

***

R9 sat in a packed library, surrounded by books that had filled its brain with insight into Vanicrast's history and the development of its people. It could understand what had happened, why the present was happening, and predict what could happen. Kaio and it would often speak about the future, and assess what to do next; it could tell that Kaio was grateful for R9's presence. Champ would visit too, not to talk, but to spar, battle and play; occasionally they would share in physical activities off of the island. R9 had seen and experienced much of Vanicrast since its creation, but there always felt like something was missing from its corrupted software.

A soft bell chimed in the other room, alerting R9 that its new program was completed. R9 rose, and walked into its laboratory, running its fingers across the steel work surfaces and the metallic robot parts it'd developed, as it advanced to its computer system. Plugging itself in, the program began automatically on its lower functions, and it immediately noted its affects. A programmed emotion filled its fictional heart: contentment.

***

"And we are coming live from outside Saviour Palace in Haula, where Prince Oxar has just been reunited with his parents, King Xavier and Queen Eleck. Reports state that after the conclusion of the seventeenth season of *Eclipse*, broadcasted illegally and hosted by Kaio, the self-named God of tournaments, the exiled Prince has been going kingdom to kingdom in search of his parents, to take his rightful place as heir to the throne," the radio host announced for the third time that afternoon. Pandora sipped her tea quietly, seated behind her wooden desk in her dimly lit office, in the Yanstag underworld.

She was glad to be home, she knew that she had enough money to leave this ill-gotten place to the rats that knocked at her door, but the idea of abandoning her old life had proved itself to be difficult. The radio in the kitchen clicked off as she took another sip of her tea.

"So, back to business," Pandora announced, as the shadowy figure exiting her kitchen, "I have family in Riodic, although I have little other reason to go there, and I have always wanted to visit Vilderton, is it true that it's a city lost in time?"

"It's true," Kaio replied, coming into the light, "I never thought I'd see this place again. How are you, by the way?"

"I'm fine," Pandora answered, "All things considered."

"All things considered," Kaio nodded, "Oxar seems to have landed on his feet too, or should I say Prince Oxar now? It is a shame that Miss Sty has disappeared though; I had wanted to check in on her too. And how about you?"

The figure sat opposite Pandora, sipped loudly before leaning forward with a smile,

"I'm fine too," Trigger answered, pushing nir hair out of nir eyes. Ne was wearing a blue flannel shirt with a long, black skirt, and nir revolvers hung loosely by nir waist,

"All things considered."

Chapter Twenty-Five
A Visit Before a War

The brittle soil beneath Kaio's feet crunched as he advanced towards the small tent. He could feel the eyes of the 'barbaric' Grothaig troops watch him as he walked towards their leader's home. Yet, none of them attempted to stop him, fearing what Kaio might do, and if Kaio spared them, what Lord Brawlax would do instead.

Kaio pushed past through the flaps, and was greeted with a strong aroma of cinnamon perfume, and the naked flesh of a pair of ladies who lay under a thick fur blanket on the floor, which scarcely covered them. Kaio sighed, rolling his eyes as he stepped over them.

"Why do you sigh?" A deep voice questioned from across the tent, the flames outlining the Minotaur Lord and his favourite elven maid.

"You know why I sigh, Brawlax," Kaio answered, "Just like you know why I am here."

"Come now," Brawlax said, before whispering to the girl to join the others under the blanket, "Don't be like that." Kaio could not resist watching the girl cross the room, before he waved his hand and summoned a screen around him and the warlord.

"Did you see this season of *Eclipse*?" Kaio questioned.

"Of course. We all did. We may be considered to be savages, but even we have televisions," Brawlax chuckled.

"And, do you still intend to fight?" Kaio asked, fearing the answer.

"Kaio, you have done great work," Brawlax began, as he leant forwards to poke the flames, "You gave the people violence, you've made the people scared of you and what you can do, but they don't fear you like they used to. They aren't horrified by what your players can do, they're disgusted. Why else would they try to sentence you?"

"Millions will die," Kaio started, but Brawlax raised his hand and silenced the 'God'.

"They will, and they will feel threatened, terrified, and horrified by what others can do. It's just a means to an end," Brawlax stated, "Your '*Eclipse*' game is a great antibiotic, but there is no cure to this disease. If I don't start the fight, someone else will, and then the circle will just start again, only *Eclipse* will be completely ineffective. My way, you'll still have a chance to help after the dust settles." Silence fell over them; as they both absorbed the others point of view.

"They hail you as a hero, you know," Kaio stated, "You died, trying to save innocent children."

"And I thank you, you have always been a good friend," Brawlax replied, "But this will happen, on my terms, or on someone else's." Kaio stood, and breathed slowly, nodding.

"It is always nice to see you, Kaio," Brawlax stated, raising and offering his hand to shake. Kaio looked at it with a sinking heart.

"It was nice to see you too,"

Kaio took the hand and shook meekly, "Rinast."

Printed in the USA
CPSIA information can be obtained
at www.ICGtesting.com
LVHW022153151123
764097LV00013B/326